ISBN 978-1-330-06592-1
PIBN 10017110

1 MONTH OF
FREE
READING

at

www.ForgottenBooks.com

By purchasing this book you are eligible for one month membership to ForgottenBooks.com, giving you unlimited access to our entire collection of over 700,000 titles via our web site and mobile apps.

To claim your free month visit:

www.forgottenbooks.com/free17110

A NOVEL.

EDITED BY

THE AUTHOR OF "EMILIA WYNDHAM,"

'TWO OLD MEN'S TALES,"

ETC. ETC.

> Queste miei carte in lieta fronte accoglie,
> Che quasi in voto à te, sacrate i'porto."
>
> TASSO.

IN THREE VOLUMES.

VOL. II.

LONDON:

HENRY COLBURN, PUBLISHER,

GREAT MARLBOROUGH STREET.

1850.

LONDON :

PRINTED BY HARRISON AND SON,
ST. MARTIN'S LANE.

ADELAIDE LINDSAY.

CHAPTER I.

THE ball, a subscription one, was to take place in the fine room of the Town Hall of D——and there, in due time, the party from Bury Hill proceeded.

Mostyn had been asked to dine, and go with them, but his Colonel had previously invited him to join his wife, lady Cecilia's party, who was one of the lady patronesses, and he could not well excuse himself from accepting it. It was Adelaide's first ball, and every thing was new and exciting to her. The long train of slowly advancing carriages, as they approached the Town Hall, whose windows, brilliantly illuminated, looked like an Aladdin's palace—the crowds assembled to witness the company arrive, their dingy garments contrasting harshly with the rustling silks and floating muslins, the coronets of flowers, and diadems of jewels, which descended from each succeeding carriage as it stopped at the entrance, and then drove rapidly away. At length the Willoughby's carriage made its way to the door, and the party alighting, proceeded up the grand staircase, lighted on either side by wax candles, each fixed into the muzzle of a musket, to the cloaking-room.

The cloaking-room was small and crowded with ladies. Some were arranging their head-dresses before the glass, while others stood impatiently behind, waiting to step into the same place as soon as vacated. It was curious to observe how much more time was taken at this employment by the elderly young ladies, than by their more juvenile companions; so much so, that a pretty accurate conclusion might have been arrived at as to their respective ages, by calculating each additional minute spent before the mirror, as a year added on to five and twenty. Some were smoothing the lace upon their dresses, or pulling out the bows, and settling the flowers. Adelaide could not help thinking of the birds preparing for the party of a certain renowned peacock. A buzz of voices arose from the whole, in which might occasionally be distinguished such exclamations as the following :—

" Where is my fan ? "

" Who *has* taken up my pocket-handkerchief ?—Allow me, if you please.—Oh, here it is !—Thank you."

" Oh, Charlotte ! I am sure my slip is below my dress," cried a third, in a voice of the deepest distress. " Do look !"

" Oh, no !—it is all right. Pray make haste ! The band has begun that darling waltz !—We shall get no partners, Jemima."

" There !—my sandal has broken ! Did you ever know anything so provoking ?"

" Well, put a pin in it !"

Then a voice from without ; some impatient brother.

" Do come along ! What *are* you about ?' &c. &c. &c.

Adelaide stood by much amused, while Miss Hawkstone was combing out her long dark curls ; at length she gave the last finishing touch, and the three ladies, accompanied by two young gentlemen of the neighbourhood, who completed their party, proceeded to the ball-room.

Adelaide was almost bewildered by the blaze of lights, the stunning music, the brilliant uniforms of the officers, and the gay dresses of the ladies, as they flew past in the giddy waltz, while the floor vibrated under their feet. She stood with Mrs. Willoughby near the entrance, for there was such a crowd standing round to look at the dancers, that they could not make much advance. Isabella was already whirled off by one of the gentlemen of their party.

"At last I have found you," said a low, sweet voice, at her elbow; "I have been watching the door-way for the last half-hour, expecting your arrival, and have not yet danced, for fear I should miss your entrée, and your first quadrille, which, I trust you have not forgotten is promised to me."

Adelaide was not likely to have done so; and the waltz having closed in one last triumphant clang, and the gasping, heated dancers dispersing about the room, Mostyn drew her hand within his arm, and led her away to secure places in the quadrille which soon began to form.

Never had Adelaide appeared to such advantage as upon this night. An air of subdued consciousness veiled the animation which usually sparkled in her eyes, giving an additional interest to her expressive features; and there was a radiance of happiness illuminating her countenance which completed the charm of her appearance. Many turned round to remark her as she passed; many were the whispered inquiries who she was? As for Mostyn himself, he regarded her with an expression of the fondest admiration.; and every word which he addressed to her, even the most indifferent, seemed absolutely steeped in tenderness.

"Some one sent me a lovely present," said Adelaide, as the quadrille proceeded, " and I do not think I need travel very far to make my thanks to the giver."

" Who is sufficiently rewarded by your wearing it," he replied, with a look of the greatest satisfaction.

" I could almost have supposed you had despatched some fairy to the West Indies," continued Adelaide, " I recognise so many of my old friends here."

" I did—and his name was—Devotion !"

" I am afraid he must have had a great deal of trouble to collect them," said Adelaide, smiling.

" Nothing," exclaimed he, passionately, "is a trouble for those one—I mean," checking himself, " that to serve you is the happiness

of my life! Do not you feel that it is?—
that it must be so, Adelaide.—Miss Lindsay, I mean?" and he looked at her with
an expression of the tenderest feeling.

Adelaide's eyes sunk beneath it; and he
continued, in a low and earnest tone:

"Ah! if I could flatter myself that my
feelings were returned, and that I dared to
tempt my fate! Enlightened by the influence of a woman I could adore, how different would my life bĕcome!—To please
her should be that aim, that purpose, which
you have so often told me I want—without
which my life is as a ship without rudder
or compass—Ah Adelaide! if considera-
tions——"

He stopped short, and Adelaide knew
not what to reply. Fortunately her vis-à-

vis here claimed her attention, and relieved her from her embarrassment. When she returned to her place at Mostyn's side, their conversation fell upon some indifferent topic. It is difficult to *renouer* such an one as Mostyn had involved himself in, when once interrupted. So they continued to talk on upon any little trifle which the ball-room suggested, till the quadrille concluded. Mostyn led his partner back at her request to Mrs. Willoughby's side.

The next quadrille she danced with one of the gentlemen who had come with them. When she returned again to her seat, she found Mrs. Willoughby had left the spot to go into the refreshment-room, and as she did not waltz, sat down to await her return, her partner being engaged, and evidently unwilling to accompany her on a voyage of discovery after her friend.

Two young officers stood just before her, and she could not avoid overhearing the following dialogue, the first words of which rivetted her attention.

" Who is the young lady with whom Mostyn is carrying on such a desperate flirtation? Have you seen her? Is she here to-night?—They were all joking him about some new flame at mess this evening —new, I suppose, since I went on leave."

" I have only just left that confounded whist-table, and I really can't tell you. Besides, I hardly know her by sight.—I suppose she is with the Bury Hill party. Who is he dancing with now ?"

" A tall, fine-looking girl in pink."

"Oh! that's Miss Hawkstone—he was amusing himself with her before this last affair; but that's all off now I suppose— even Mostyn could not carry ou more than one flirtation in the same house at once —that would never pay!"

"Cut each other's throats, you think? Poor Miss Hawkstone, I pity her!"

"Oh, I don't think she minds!—She is taking up with old Grey, they say."

" And has sense enough to prefer a colonel to a captain.—But this young lady we were speaking of—is she pretty?"

"Very much so indeed. I saw her at a pic-nic some weeks ago, and I thought her one of the very sweetest girls I ever saw. — But ladies look so dif- ferent in their bonnets. I don't think

I should know her if I were to see her again."

" Does he mean to propose this time ?"

"Propose !—Mostyn propose !—He is not quite such a fool as all that comes to ! No, no—trust me !—he'll never marry a girl without money; and I am told that Miss Lindsay has not a penny."

" Why. Mostyn can't be so very badly off, and. I do not see why he should not please himself some day.—They were saying he was regularly in for it this time; and she appears from all accounts to be such a very charming girl."

" My dear fellow !—I joined at the same time as Mostyn; and I can assure you that he has been 'in for it,' as you call it, a hundred and ninety-nine times at the very least, and has always managed to get out of it as yet."

" Well, he's a deuced lucky fellow to be so fortunate !   But he will be caught and landed high and dry some day yet—mark my words !"

" Well, he's as nice a fellow as ever lived, and I sincerely hope he may escape such a terrible fate. — But don't you want to dance?   Come along, and I'll introduce you to a nice little girl for a partner."

And they walked off together.

Adelaide's feelings during these last few minutes may be imagined rather than described.   Surprise, incredulity, humiliation, and indignation by turns took possession of her mind.   Was it possible !   Could Cap-

tain Mostyn be the heartless flirt she
had just heard described?—Was she so
miserably deceived? — Could he have
been trifling with her so recklessly all
this time.

Oh, no, no!—they were mistaken in him.
How could she reconcile such an account
with the acknowledged uprightness and
truthfulness of his conduct in every other
respect? She repeated to herself the broken
and impassioned sentences he had poured
into her ear not half an hour ago. He
might have laughed, and talked, and flirted
before; but surely, never could he have
spoken to others as he had spoken to
her!— And again, every little incident
of their acquaintance — each daily increasing proof of his tenderness towards

herself, passed in rapid review before her
memory.

Oh, how did she feel the want of a
mother, a sympathizing sister, that she
might tell them all, all! and ask their
advice and guidance. Mrs. Willoughby, it
was true, was as kind to her as any mother
or sister could be, but still, she was but a
friend of not many weeks' standing, and Adelaide felt a repugnance to mention her per-
plexity to her. If what she had just overheard was actually true, she might think
her so foolish! so conceited! to suppose
Captain Mostyn's attentions signified any
thing more than that civility which he would
pay to any other agreeable girl, more espe-
cially, if before her arrival they had been
devoted to Miss Hawkstone, who, from

what she had gathered, evidently had thought but slightly of them; more sensible in this respect than herself, as she bitterly considered—if—if—it was all true!

No, she would consult no one. If she had been deceiving herself all this time—if he had been only amusing himself with her, as his brother officers seemed to believe, she would soon find it out, and drive him for ever from her thoughts!

But whilst she made this resolution, the choking sensation in her throat, and the sudden pang of pain in her heart, might have warned her how hard would be the struggle.

Mrs. Willoughby at length returned to

her seat, and finding Adelaide unengaged, introduced her to an acquaintance for the next quadrille. Mostyn was their vis-à-vis. He could not but observe an alteration in her manner towards himself, as the quadrille brought them together—a seriousness and abstraction which she found it utterly impossible to command.

"Let me take you down to supper," said he, entreatingly, as he crossed to her side in one of the figures.

"Very well," replied she, coldly, and turned again to her partner.

As soon as the quadrille was ended, Mostyn came up to claim Adelaide's promise, and they both went down in silence to the supper room. It was so crowded that it was impossible to find places, indeed hardly entrance, and Mostyn proposed that they should wait in the comparatively cool ante-room, till the throng around the supper table began to disperse a little. Adelaide consented, and they seated themselves on a sofa, near the door-way.

" How have you enjoyed your first ball?" began he, after a little silence; and then, without waiting for a reply, continued,— " For my part, I have never amused myself less!—Wearied with talking to, and dancing with, people I could not avoid asking, though I wished them at the world's end for preventing me from being where alone I am happy," and he raised his eyes, half-timidly, to her face; " how could it be otherwise!"

"I do not know how it is," he went on, almost impatiently, "but these last few weeks, I can find no pleasure in what formerly I used to enjoy.—I used to like balls and parties, and all that sort of thing, more, perhaps, than *you* would consider quite sensible; but now all seems to me 'stale, flat, and unprofitable.' Can you help me to account for this?—Is it that when all one's thoughts are engrossed by one object, every thing else seems to lose its interest?"

"If one *had* one engrossing object, I should imagine it very likely," replied she, quietly.

He bit his lip.

"Then you do not give me credit .for— you do not think I am capable of being so absorbed.—Do you think me, then, so very trifling."

" Indeed, Captain Mostyn, I never said so. You must know your own character far better than I can pretend to do."

He looked down; and then said, with much feeling,—

" I had flattered myself that by this time you *did* know my character a little—that you had taken some slight interest in it. But I see that I have been much mistaken; and that all I have ever said to you has been heard with merely that attention which Miss Lindsay would be too polite to refuse to the most indifferent of her acquaintance."

" Oh, Captain Mostyn!"

She could say no more; but how did she long to tell him what she had over-

heard, and hear a denial of the calumny
from his own lips. But to repeat to him a
conversation of his brother officers, which
was certainly never intended to reach his
ears, and which had so accidentally come
to her knowledge, would have been an
indiscretion, of which Adelaide was indeed
incapable, independent of any further consideration.

" Oh, Captain Mostyn!" was all she said,
but what did not those few words express?

He passionately seized her hand, exclaiming with earnest tenderness,

" Oh, Adelaide! May I flatter myself——" Then, as if recollecting where
they were, he let it fall, and added hurriedly, " that—that—you condescend to
feel a little interest for me?"

Before she could reply, Mrs. Willoughby
came up, and interrupted the conversation
by inquiring whether they had been in to
supper, and requesting they would lose no
time, as it was getting late, and Mr. Willoughby particularly objected to the horses
being kept waiting.

Adelaide declined taking any refresh-
ment, and followed Mostyn and Mrs. Willoughby to the cloaking-room. As he was
tenderly assisting her with her shawl their
eyes met. They seemed to understand each
other better than ever, after their little
quarrel, and Adelaide felt certain that she
could not mistake the loving and truthful
expression of those dark eyes as they looked
into her own, nor the almost involuntary
pressure of the arm that lay within his, as

he led her to the carriage, as if it would entreat her not to doubt him. Her confidence restored, she reached Bury Hill, and once more happy and satisfied, laid her innocent head upon her pillow.

CHAPTER II.

THE next morning, when Adelaide came down to breakfast, a letter from Mr. Brown lay by the side of her plate. They had continued to correspond very regularly, but that which, before her arrival at Bury Hill, she had so anxiously desired, was now the farthest from her wishes, and. every letter which she received from him, was opened with a feeling of dread, lest it should contain the intelligence that he had succeeded at length in his endeavours, and had found her a situation as governess.

She broke the seal, and read as follows:—

" MY DEAR ADELAIDE,

"I have at length met with a situation that I can, with the utmost confidence, recommend you to accept. The lady is a very accomplished as well as excellent woman, and you will find in her a very interesting companion, as well as a kind friend. There are only two little girls to teach, so that you will not find your task very fatiguing; and she is most liberal in the remuneration she offers you.

"In short, my dear child, I consider myself very fortunate in the result of my search, as there is nothing left to desire for you.

"You will write me, by return of post, what day you will arrive at your grand-mother's; and I will meet you there, and go with you to introduce you in person to Lady Kynnaston. She lives in the Isle of Wight.

"Ever, my dear Adelaide,

"Your affectionate friend

"and guardian,

"WILLIAM BROWN."

Adelaide finished her breakfast in silence;

then rose from the table, and putting the letter into Mrs. Willoughby's hand, left the room.

"Now," thought Mrs. Willoughby, after hastily reading the letter, and as leisurely folding it again, "Now matters must come to a termination! This will bring Captain Mostyn to the point—nothing could turn out more fortunately or *àpropos!* Adelaide shall be married from this house—what a lovely bride she will make! Poor Charles! However, the sooner it is all over the better. As long as she continues un-married, he will still nourish hope in spite of himself—and the sooner she becomes irrevo-cably another's, the sooner he will recover."

She rose, and followed Adelaide to her room.

Adelaide was sitting in an arm-chair, her head thrown back upon the cushion, while her hands were playing mechanically with the chain of her watch. She started to her feet when the door opened.

"Well, my dear," said Mrs. Willoughby, as she entered, "I must congratulate you, I suppose, upon the subject of this letter; for I conclude you will think it advisable to accept the offer.

"Indeed I do not see upon what pretext I could refuse it," replied Adelaide.

"Nor do I," said Mrs. Willoughby.

She could hardly forbear smiling the while, when she thought of the little probability there was of the young Kynnastons ever benefitting by her instructions.

"I think this family is probably related

to one of the same name with which my
brother is intimately acquainted. Possibly
it may be the very same. They are people
of the highest respectability. Well, my
love, we shall all miss you very much, for
indeed you have endeared yourself to all of
us—I hardly know who amongst us will
regret you most."

Adelaide could not speak, for again that
choking sensation returned in her throat.
She was disappointed in Mrs. Willoughby's
manner of receiving the intelligence; she
had expected more apparent sorrow at her
departure; that she would perhaps have
divined why such a departure must be so
particularly painful to herself. If all this
time Mrs. Willoughby had not observed
what was going on between Captain Mostyn

and herself, would it not argue that there had been, after all, nothing unusual in his conduct? and that her inexperience in the ways of the world had misled her? Again, the words of his brother officer rang in her ears—all her torturing doubts returned. He, perhaps, would regret her no more than Mrs. Willoughby appeared to do. She felt lonely and deserted, as if no one cared for her. When one is unhappy, one is often unjust.

Mrs. Willoughby perceived her emotion, and partly guessed its cause.

"My dearest child," said she, laying her hand with caressing tenderness upon her head, "have you nothing in your heart that you would tell to your mother if you had one?—Consider me in that light,

Adelaide. If affection is a title to confidence, I do not think, my love, you would easily find one who felt more of it towards you than I do."

These soothing words fell like balm upon the slightly embittered feelings of Adelaide's heart. The tears dropped from her eyes, and to conceal them she bent forwards and sunk her brow upon her kind friend's shoulder.

Mrs. Willoughby continued, "You cannot suppose, my dear girl, that I have been *quite* blind to what has been going on these last few weeks.—I do not *know* what your own feelings are, but I should give you credit for a rather unusual degree of obduracy if you have been quite proof against the evident affection and admiration you have inspired in a certain quarter. Lift up your head, dear, and let me *see* what I suppose you have not the courage to let me *hear*."

.She gently raised Adelaide's head from her shoulder as she spoke. The bright blush, and eyes cast down, were any thing but refutations of the impeachment.

"Oh, Mrs. Willoughby," she said, in a voice so low that it was almost a whisper, "much as I love you, I cannot say that it is the thoughts of leaving you alone, that occasions my sorrow." Then, after a slight pause, she resumed, "I have so much wished to tell you all—but I could not find the courage—I was afraid you might think me foolish—for these matters," with a timid smile, "often seem so ridiculous to standers-by—I was afraid you might think me so very foolish—particularly since what I heard last night."

"What did you hear last night?"

Adelaide related to her the substance of the dialogue she had overheard in the ball-room. When she had concluded; "My dear," said Mrs. Willoughby, "I think far too well of Captain Mostyn to believe it possible that he is only trifling with you. I do not mean to say that he is not inclined to be what is generally termed a flirt; I have heard him accused of this before. He flirted with Isabella; he flirted with Miss Bellair; he may have flirted with numbers of girls before, for what I know, and very likely has; he is very lively and animated, and a general favourite. I do not mean to say that I approve of such conduct on his part ; for to say the least of it, I think it very silly, and it is the one defect which I have observed in his otherwise charming and engaging character; and one that I have not the slightest doubt a real and worthy attachment will cure him of, for ever.

"But how different has been his conduct towards you than that towards any other young lady of my acquaintance !—To you he has shown every mark of a *true* attachment. Such evident delight in your society! Such an uneasy restlessness when away from your side! Such tenderness and admiration expressed in look and tone !—No, my dear, do not do him such an injustice—do not think you have been foolish—do not think you have given away your heart to one who

had not previously given you all his own.—
Captain Mostyn loves you!"

"Thank you, dearest, dearest, Mrs. Willoughby!" exclaimed Adelaide, kissing her
hand, joy and happiness beaming from every
feature. We often feel more grateful for a
confirmed hope, than for the most magnificent of gifts. "Now I will write to Mr.
Brown, and accept Lady Kynnaston's offer,
and fix the day for my departure."

"Wait till to night, my dear ; the post
does not go out till late—you need not be
in such a hurry!"

Mrs. Willoughby felt sure that Captain
Mostyn would call that afternoon, and that
an explanation would then take place between the lovers, which might possibly
occasion an alteration in Adelaide's plans.

She now left the room, and Adelaide, who felt a desire to be alone, soon afterwards took her paper and drawing-box into the garden, with the intention of finishing, before her departure, a sketch of the house and pleasure-grounds which Captain Mostyn had asked her to take for him.

She was in a tumult of contradictory feelings, now all joy at the confirmation, which she had received from Mrs. Willoughby, of her own persuasions, and now sad at the thoughts of the approaching separation, and the sorrow which it would occasion to Mostyn. She had made no secret of her plans to him, and he had long been made aware how she was situated with regard to pecuniary matters, and of the necessity there was that she should contribute by her own exertions to her maintenance. He was far above thinking the less of her for the position which her father's misfortunes would compel her to occupy, and had admired her all the more for her honourable and independent spirit. She had, therefore, none of the distressing doubts which might have tormented another in her situation, as to what effect such a change in her place in society might produce upon his feelings and intentions.

CHAPTER III.

MRS. WILLOUGHBY sat writing in t drawing-room. She heard the sound of horses' feet, the door-bell rang, and Captain Mostyn walked in.

"I have brought a book for Frederick, Mrs. Willoughby;" said he, coming up to the table where she sat; "one that will be of great use to him in his studies, I think, if you can persuade him to read it. It is a pity he is so inclined to be idle, for he is a clever fellow."

Some conversation ensued upon the education of boys in general, and of Frederick in particular; but Captain Mostyn kept playing with the tassel of his sword the whole time—he had been on duty that morning, and had only just left drill—turning round quickly every time the door chanced to open, to resume his former position with an air of disappointment, showing that he was not taking much interest in the discourse. At last :—

"I hope Miss Lindsay was not knocked up by the ball, last night;" he said.

"Not in the least. She was down to breakfast at the usual time this morning, and looked as well as she always does."

Mrs. Willoughby had determined to say nothing of Mr. Brown's letter, but to leave the communication of its contents entirely to Adelaide.

" I saw her pass by this window towards the summer-house, with her sketch-book, about half an hour ago."

Mostyn looked towards the open window, and began turning his cap round and round in his hand.

At last he said abruptly :

" Did you see Lady Cecilia last night ? She says there is no such thing as a white moss rose, and we had a bet upon the subject.—I know there are some in your garden. Will you

allow me to gather one or two, **Mrs.**
Willoughby ?"

" Oh, certainly—as many as you like;"
replied she, laughing ; " You will find them
in the rosary, to the right of the fountain."

" Thank you; I remember perfectly,"
said he, rising, and stepping through the
open window upon the lawn.

Mrs. Willoughby smiled again, as she
watched him walking off in exactly the
opposite direction to the rosary.

" He thinks he shall find the white rose
in the summer-house, I suspect," thought she;
and with an air of satisfaction settled herself
once more down to her writing.

Captain Mostyn dawdled up the lawn,
whistling an air from the last new opera, till

he was out of sight of the drawing-room window, he then quickened his pace, and approached the summer-house.

This little summer-house was quite at the farther end of the pleasure grounds. In front of it was a tiny pool of crystal water, full of gold and silver fish, and surrounded by a rock border, enamelled with yellow and crimson cistus, and plants of that description; behind, it was sheltered by a thick shrubbery of yew and laurel; it was covered with creepers, and commanded a very pretty view of the house and flower-gardens.

Mostyn walked softly up to the little window on one side, for the turf prevented his footstep from being heard, and looked in.

Adelaide was seated on a bench before the rustic table; her large straw hat had fallen at her feet, and her rich and golden curls shaded her face, which was bent towards the paper upon which she was drawing. She seemed absorbed in her occupation. Mostyn remained observing her for a little time, and then walked round to the entrance. The shadow thrown by his figure roused her attention and she looked up.

"You were very intent upon your employment," said he, coming in, and seating himself upon the bench beside her. "I have been watching you for the last five minutes through that little window, and you never once looked up."

"Have you, really," replied she; "I

never heard you—and you quite startled me with your silent shadow upon my drawing-paper. — I suppose it was as you say, that I was so occupied with my sketch.—I so much wish to finish it before I go."

"Before you go? Adelaide!—What can you mean?"

"Did not Mrs. Willoughby tell you?" said she, in a low voice, and again bending so low over her drawing that it was impossible to see the expression of her countenance.

"Tell me?—No—she told me nothing— What do you mean?"

"Only that I had a letter from Mr. Brown this morning, to say that he had at last succeeded in his search; and that I

am to go as soon as possible to Lady Kynnaston's."

" Lady Kynnaston!—Who on earth is
Lady Kynnaston ?"

" The lady whose children I am to
teach."

" Oh, Adelaide ! you can't go—you are
not going !" in a voice of excited entreaty.

"Indeed, I must, Captain Mostyn,—you
know how I am situated."

" Mrs. Willoughby will not allow you to
leave her.—She loves you too much—she
cannot spare you !"

" I have spoken to Mrs. Willoughby," said
Adelaide, sadly.

" Then *I* cannot spare you !" cried he
impetuously.

" Oh, Adelaide ! What can I do without

you ?—Don't go—don't go. Do not you care to leave me?" His eye became humid with emotion, as he uttered these broken sentences with passionate, imploring tenderness.

She could make no answer, but the tears which she had hitherto restrained, now fell in silence, one after the other, from her long, dark eyelashes. He took one of her hands in his, and passed the other round her form. Her head sank upon his shoulder, and he pressed a kiss upon her forehead.

" Oh, Mostyn !" she said, " I have been so unhappy!"

" So unhappy, my dearest! What could have made my Adelaide unhappy, except it were the thoughts of our separation ?"

" Oh, no ! It was not that alone !"

"What then, my love ?—Tell me all."

"It was—" she began hesitatingly, "that
from a conversation I accidentally overheard,
I feared that after all, perhaps, you did not
seriously care for me—that I had been mistaken—that—that—" She had raised her
head from his shoulder almost immediately,
and now looked up into his face, with an expression of the most child-like and confiding
affection, and as if she would ask his pardon
for her momentary distrust; but he appeared
so confused—so troubled—as avoiding
her eye, his face grew deadly pale, that
she stopped short, and knew not how to
proceed.

At last he said, in an indistinct and
hesitating voice :

"Perhaps I should have told you before,

which now I can no longer conceal from you
—that I am poor.—I have little besides my
pay. I could not be so selfish as to ask
you to share my poverty.—I never for one
moment thought of it."

Adelaide immediately released herself
from the arm which still encircled her figure,
and rising, said, " Then it is indeed well
that we part so soon, since it must now be
for ever !"

A woman's pride stifled for the moment
her affection ! That she should have been
betrayed into · such a confession as she had
just made ; and, as it were, accepting a hand
which it had never been his intention to
offer, overpowered her with shame and confusion. She loathed the hand he had so
fondly caressed—that one kiss burnt like

a brand into her brow, desecrated by the avowal he had just made.

" He had never for one moment thought of it !"

Thought of what ? Thought of her in the sacred character of wife !

Could then her conduct be accused of such levity, as to deserve that she should be subjected to treatment, which she could now only regard as insulting ? Would he have ventured so far with Miss Hawk-stone ?

Oh ! No, no ! It was her poverty—her unprotected situation ! — No father—no brother !—Oh, if the earth would open and swallow her up as she stood !

She attempted to leave the arbour, but he detained her, exclaiming,—

"Adelaide! stop;—do not leave me thus —Why should we part?—Why should not we continue to love on as we have been doing?"

"No, Captain Mostyn!" said she, indignation flashing from her eyes; "to you it may be easy to love here to day, and there to-morrow, wherever fortune and your fancy may lead you.—But I cannot play fast and loose with my affections.—I loved you as truly and sincerely as I believed you loved me. But now, I do so no longer;— your conduct has been its own cure—I cannot love where I no longer esteem."

"Oh, Adelaide!" cried he, in a voice of agony; "do not say that—I cannot bear it!" He again seized her hand. "How have I deserved it? What have I done more than others ?—— You are unjust and cruel !"

" Unjust and cruel !—Is it unjust to feel some indignation ?—Was it right—was it honourable, to extort from me the avowal of an affection, which, had I known you as I now know you, I never would have cherished—which I would have died rather than have confessed ? Oh, Captain Mostyn ! if your sister had been treated by another as you have treated me, what would have been your feelings ?—I am *ashamed* of having loved you !" She covered her face with her hands.

He sunk again upon the seat, in great emotion. " Oh, Adelaide !" cried he, " Let my love for you plead some excuse for my conduct."

"If you had truly loved me, you never would so selfishly have given me pain, for the sake of affording yourself a few weeks' miserable amusement—you never would have done all in your power to secure an affection which——" She stopped; emotion choked her utterance. Then she hurriedly added,—

"What am I saying ?—Leave me, Captain Mostyn !"

"Adelaide ! Adelaide ! Will you drive me from you thus ?—If you will not believe in my affection, at least believe in my contrition." His head sank upon the table— he seemed overpowered by his feelings.

"Ah, Mostyn," she said, "I do not mean to reproach you—I have already said more than I ought—more than I intended. Per-

haps it is pride that makes me feel so
bitterly—a woman's pride, which you cannot
understand!—But if, indeed, you grieve
for what has passed—for the anguish—the
guiltless shame—the confusion which you
have occasioned me—the next time you are
tempted to try your power upon a woman's
heart, think on one who could have lived to
have made you happy, and choose a more
experienced victim!"

She once more moved to depart.

"Stay, Adelaide!" cried he, catching her
by the dress, "Stay yet one moment, and
tell me.—Will you—will you accept me,
poor as I am?—I have little besides
my pay, but many have lived happily on
less."

"No, Captain Mostyn!—It shall never

be said that your compassion led you to take a step which your prudence condemned!—And now, farewell!" reaching him her hand; "Let us put an end to this most painful scene. Pray leave me, Captain Mostyn."

"Say you forgive me!" said he, pressing that hand to his heart, while the veins stood out like cords upon his forehead, and his swollen eyelids gave witness to the sincerity of his emotion.

"Forgive you!" she replied with returning tenderness; "from my heart I forgive you, Mostyn!"

He longed to catch her to his breast, but dared not.—He still hesitated.

"Go, go!" she urged, almost imperatively.

He stooped for his cap which lay on the

floor at his feet, and left the summer-house
—and thus they parted.

Adelaide sunk upon the bench he had so
lately quitted. Her arms, which lay crossed
upon the little table, concealed her face;
she was perfectly motionless, and no sound
proceeded from her lips. She seemed crushed
beneath the weight of bitter thoughts and
feelings which crowded upon her mind. [Too
much stunned to analyze them, she could
only suffer passively.

At length she raised her head, and passed
her hand languidly across her brow; she
looked pale, exhausted, and weary, as one
who had endured some torturing pain; and
her eyes were heavy. If she might then
have had her wish, she would have fallen
asleep, and never have awakened in this

world again! So feel the young in their first heart's agony!—They think that life is over for them; life with its love,—its trust, its joy,—its hope! But it is not so. Time, the beneficent, bears us forward on its healing wings, and we forget!

Adelaide rose from her seat. The drawing she had been finishing with feelings of such exquisite, though mingled happiness, lay before her. She never could bear she thought, to look upon it again; and taking it up, she tore it slowly in pieces, and scattered it to the winds. She then went to the little fountain and bathed her brow and eyes in its cold and refreshing waters; then tying on her hat she walked towards the house; she met no one, and reached her own room unobserved.

When once there, she bolted her door, and again sat down to consider; but thought was too distressing! Her brow slightly contracted for a moment, and she shook her head with almost an impatient gesture, as if she would drive away some painful image, —she could not think!

She reached pen and ink, and began a letter to Mr. Brown. Hardly had she written two lines when there was a gentle knock at the door. Adelaide rose to open it, and Mrs. Willoughby came in.

" Here you are, my dear!" said she, " I could not imagine what had become of you. —How tired you look!—What, my love, is the matter?"

" I am writing to Mr. Brown," said Adelaide, evading the question.

" To say that circumstances have arisen to prevent you accepting his offer ?—Eh, my dear ?"

" No," said Adelaide ; " I am writing to say I shall come ; and I am only waiting to know at what hour to-morrow it will be most convenient to you, for me to leave you."

" To leave us ! — My dearest girl ! — What is all this about ?—Have you seen Captain Mostyn ?"

" Yes."

" Did you tell him of Mr. Brown's letter "

" I did," replied Adelaide, in a low voice.

" Well."

" Dearest, dearest Mrs. Willoughby !" in a tone of the most affecting entreaty, " ask me no further !—Allow me only to say, that

I am now most grateful to this necessity for leaving Bury Hill."

" I understand you perfectly, my dear, —say no more," said Mrs. Willoughby, pressing the cold hand which had taken her own. She was too really kind and sympathising to feel hurt at a silence, which another might have felt as a want of confidence. "*After all her kindness!*" and how inexpressibly grateful did Adelaide feel for her forbearance! She could not enter into any explanation without criminating Mostyn, and she had loved him too dearly to bear that any one should blame him but herself. That, alas! she could not forbear doing!—Her own upright and honourable mind shrunk with peculiar abhorrence from what she could not but consider as conduct, on his part, so reprehensible and unprincipled; and it was the consideration that having forfeited her esteem, she *ought* no longer to love him, that gave her more anguish than any other feeling.

Mrs. Willoughby now arranged with Adelaide the time for her departure, which she persuaded her to postpone for a couple of days; indeed, had she put her original plan into execution, Mr. Brown could not have received her letter in time to meet her at G——. A servant was to escort her there, for Mrs. Willoughby would not hear of her travelling alone.

" And now, my love, I will leave you to finish your letter," said Mrs. Willoughby; " I *need* not tell you how grieved I shall be to part with you. I *cannot* tell you how much I approve and admire you." She kissed her upon the forehead, and hastily left the room.

CHAPTER IV.

MRS. WILLOUGHBY was extremely per-
plexed. That something must have gone
wrong between Adelaide and Captain Mostyn she could not doubt; but as is often the
case when things do not turn out according
to one's wishes and anticipations, she felt
convinced that there must be some sad mistake or mismanagement at the bottom.—

" When two young people love each other, and there is no opposition made upon the part of their friends, what should hinder them from marrying?" thought she.

Adelaide's evident repugnance to enter into any particulars, precluded all hope of any explanation on that side, she could only trust that Mostyn might be more communicative, and that she should finally be able to put all to rights again between them; and it was, therefore, with no small satisfaction that she heard the next day, while working in her sitting-room, that Captain Mostyn had called, and was waiting to see her.

She found him leaning against the mantelpiece, looking pale and jaded. He started when she came in, and shaking hands with her, muttered some trifling remark upon the weather; he seemed disturbed and confused, as if having much that he wished to say, he could not find courage to begin. A few more common-place sentences passed between them, upon that peculiarly English subject. How do foreigners contrive to get on without it ?

"Yes, it certainly feels very close," said Mrs. Willoughby; "it looks like thunder— it may possibly account for Adelaide's indisposition; she has had a violent head-ache ever since yesterday afternoon."

"Has she? I wanted to ask—oh! Mrs. Willoughby! tell me—how is she?" interrupted Mostyn in a hurried, eager manner.

"Indeed, not at all well," replied she, in a grave tone ; and then added pointedly,

"She was sitting drawing for a long time in the summer-house yesterday—I do not know whether that might have had any thing to do with her indisposition."

"Miss Lindsay, no doubt, has acquainted you with what did take place in the summer-house," said Mostyn, looking down.

"Indeed she has told me nothing—she merely said that 'now she was very grateful that she had a pretext for leaving Bury Hill.'"

Mostyn made no reply; his eyes were still fixed upon the carpet.

Mrs. Willoughby continued,

"My dear Captain Mostyn, will you allow me as a friend of your mother's to at once and openly address you upon the subject of which I see your thoughts are full, and of which you cannot suppose me to be wholly ignorant; as certainly for the last few weeks you have not shown the least wish to conceal your feelings from even the most casual observer.—I feel sure that some misunderstanding must have arisen between you and Miss Lindsay, and am naturally very anxious that nothing which the interposition of a mutual friend could remove, should separate two young people who seem formed for each other."

The colour flew to Captain Mostyn's temples, as he replied, his eyes still bent upon the ground,

"I have acted very reprehensively—very foolishly"—he paused; then suddenly looking up, he continued,

"Mrs. Willoughby, since she has been so

generous as to avoid relating how inexcu-
sably I have been acting towards her, I
will myself tell you, that she—that you
too, I perceive—had given me credit for
more principle, more understanding than I
deserved."

"What am I to understand, Captain
Mostyn—you surely would not have me
believe, that all this time you have been
offering to Adelaide attentions, that without *in*tentions no father would allow?"

"That my attachment has carried me
beyond the bounds of prudence, I must
with the deepest contrition confess. Adelaide—I mean Miss Lindsay—discovered
yesterday that I did not contemplate, what
she had with so much reason expected."

Mrs. Willoughby arose and walked towards

the window. She felt too indignant to speak. The sincere and devoted attachment of Latimer, the pain which she well knew he was with such manly fortitude enduring—Adelaide's former radiant happiness—her present blighted appearance and silent suffering, rushed upon her mind—all proceeding from a want of common principle in one man!—But for him all might have turned out so well—all have been so happy!

She turned to Captain Mostyn, who remained still seated, his head leaning upon his hand, and said bitterly,

"You do not know what mischief you have occasioned!"

"I have deserved your indignation—I know it.—But let me explain to you—not

in extenuation of my conduct, but as a
reason—that I am, what the world in general would consider a poor man—and I
have seen so much misery attending upon
unions contracted under such circumstances,
that I had made a resolution never to enter
into any, which would preclude either party
from enjoying those conveniences and luxuries
to which they had formerly been accustomed."

"Every man, Captain Mostyn, does well
and wisely to form his plan of life according to his own ideas of happiness; and, so
long as it does not interfere with that of
another, to act in accordance with it.—It
is not your *prudence* that I blame."

"I understand you perfectly, Mrs. Willoughby," said he, sadly, "and I fear that I

have so much sunk in your opinion, that you will hardly advocate my cause, in that which I have deeply at heart."

"Go on," said she with greater kindness in her manner. She was touched by the deep feeling in his tones and expression.

"Though I am what most would consider poor, yet without culpable imprudence, without entailing beggary upon my wife and family, I might marry—I could make up an income of about £500, and my prospects eventually are good.—And now, Mrs. Willoughby," continued he, with increasing earnestness, "having explained to you my circumstances, will you stand my friend? Will you speak to Adelaide? Will you prevail upon her to forgive what has passed —to accept a hand which is offered to her,

with all the devotion, all the affection, all
the sincerity of which man's heart is capable ?
—Ask her to see me once more ?"

" I will do your errand with the greatest
pleasure—Shall I speak to her at once?"

"Oh ! immediately, I entreat of you, and
I will await her answer here."

Mrs. Willoughby immediately went to
Adelaide's room, who was engaged in pre-
parations for her departure. She could not
remain still—she could not fix her attention
upon anything. Active exertion was all
of which she was capable.

 Mrs. Willoughby came in. Adelaide
arose from the box she was packing.

" Captain Mostyn is here, my dear."

Adelaide started and coloured.

"He has sent me as an ambassador to you."

Adelaide made no reply, and Mrs. Willoughby continued,

" He has told me all, with the greatest frankness, and has sent me to beg that you will see him once again—that you will overlook and forgive what has so justly offended you—and in short, my dear, that you will accept his hand."

" Oh Mrs. Willoughby, how can I ?" exclaimed Adelaide, " what is there in his circumstances that should make that which was imprudent yesterday, prudent to-day ?"

" I do not think there will be the least imprudence in your marrying, my dear, provided you love each other sufficiently to find more happiness in very moderate cir-

cumstances shared together, than in enjoying luxuries apart. Captain Mostyn has
just told me that his prospects are good,
and that his present income amounts to
£500 a-year."

"So much!" said Adelaide in a tone of
touching reproach; "and yet until yesterday
—until he thought that I expected it, he
never thought of making me his wife!—and
can he suppose that I will now accept a
hand, which not inclination, but a feeling of
honour, perhaps— compassion! bids him
offer?—Oh, Mrs. Willoughby, he little knows
me!"

"Indeed, Adelaide, you do him hardly
justice. He loves you, I am sure."

"He may think so for the moment," she
replied—"indeed that he really does so is

my only consolation. But suppose he were to repent!—to regret those luxuries and enjoyments which he now offers to sacrifice for my sake?—Were I to accept him, imagine *then* what would be my own feelings! How could I endure the thought that inwardly he might be reproaching me for having drawn him into an engagement, which his own better judgment condemned! Drawn him into an engagement!—Oh, Mrs. Willoughby!"

"Do not you suppose, my dear, that to be married to such a woman as you are, would compensate ten thousand fold for any such paltry luxuries as he might have to relinquish?" exclaimed her friend.

" *He* did not think so, yesterday," replied Adelaide.—" Beside," continued she, colouring deeply, "remember my own situation, dearest Mrs. Willoughby—any independence would be a gain to me—Consider to what suspicions I might expose myself."

There was a slight pause, and then Mrs. Willoughby said,

"Will you not see him—he wishes to see you—he is waiting for you down stairs."

"No—no—no. I cannot—I will not—I dare not see him," exclaimed Adelaide in great agitation.—"He might persuade me! We are so easily persuaded when our own deceitful wishes go hand in hand with the persuader—and I know I am right!— Oh, Mrs. Willoughby!" said she, her fortitude at length giving way, "I thought I loved him no longer!—I ought to love him no

longer !—How wrong !—How foolish !——"
She sunk into a chair quite overcome, and
tears, bitter tears, fell through the fingers
which concealed her eyes.

"My love," said Mrs. Willoughby, in a
voice of the tenderest sympathy, "you are
not wrong!—you are not foolish!—it is
most natural! That heart must indeed be
steeped in pride, and hardened by resentment, that could at once change affection
into indifference—I will return to him
with your answer.—But what shall I say?
Give me some message."

"Tell him," said Adelaide, "that I can
give him no other answer than I did yesterday—and tell him, dear Mrs. Willoughby
—that I shall never think of him with
resentment or bitterness."

"But suppose he insists upon seeing you?"

"Then tell him that it is my last request that he will not think of it; it would pain me very much, and be quite useless. And now, my dearest Mrs. Willoughby—my almost mother—give me the satisfaction of hearing that you think I am right," taking her hand, and looking up into her face.

"Quite right, my love.—I think you are quite right." She bent forward and kissed that imploring, tear-stained countenance; then leaving her, descended again to the drawing-room.

She paused a few moments, before she opened the door, to collect her thoughts. Pleasure was uppermost—pleasure that the field was once more open to her brother;

that there was again a chance of his ultimate success; that he might still be as
happy as he deserved.

" For in time," thought she, " Adelaide
will recover this first attachment, and ap-
preciate still more, from the experience
under which she is now suffering, a love so
true, so devoted, so unselfish as that of
Charles."

She had done her duty, all that could be
expected from her, and felt no inclination
to exert her influence—even had she been
less persuaded than she was, of the pro-
priety of Adelaide's feelings—to induce her
to alter her determination. Had Captain
Mostyn really hoped to have failed in his
application, he could not have chosen a
fitter messenger.

In the meanwhile, Mostyn had been pacing up and down the room in which he had been left. His feelings of excitement and tenderness had somewhat abated, now that the dread reality of marriage stared him in the face, and that he had leisure to contemplate all the difficulties to which he and Adelaide might possibly be exposed in their union. He loved and admired her, it is true, far more than any woman he had ever been acquainted with; and had he been wealthy, would never for one moment have hesitated in asking her to become his wife; at the same time he did not possess the courage to embark without trepidation in a life of comparative self-denial. Moving from place to place; quartered now here, now there; his fancy perpetually engaged

with some new flirtation, as ephemeral as
the one before, he had little faith in an
enduring, self-sustaining attachment; and
had been utterly careless of inflicting suffering, believing, that when the day of parting
should come, it would be as transient on the
lady's side, as on his own; and circum-
stanced as he was, he had never, in any
instance, contemplated such a catastrophe,
as the usual termination to a mutual affection,—a proposal of marriage.. He had
now been led to take this step from a
mingled feeling of affection, contrition, and
honour; and awaited. Mrs. Willoughby's
return hardly knowing which he most desired, a refusal or an acceptal. Mrs. Willoughby at length came in, and delivered
Adelaide's answer.

With the sometimes strange perversity of
human nature, now that his fate was decided—that the choice no longer lay in his
power—that she had so positively refused
even to see him again, his wavering incli-
nations were at once decided. That prudence, which had previously led him to
neglect securing such happiness whilst in
his power, now appeared to him the greatest
folly. All Adelaide's charms and beauty,
her noble character, and above all, her
affection for himself, rose to his thoughts,
illuminated with a brighter radiance than
ever; and all this he had neglected to make
his own!—he had sacrificed to a moral
cowardice—to the fear of his comrades'
ridicule—to the dread of a few paltry de-
privations.

" Go to her again," cried he, " tell her I must and will see her again."

" It is useless," replied Mrs. Willoughby. " Adelaide's last request to you is, that you will desist from any such attempt, which would only give her useless pain, since her mind is quite made up upon the subject. She returns to her grandmother to-morrow. —She desired me to tell you that she will never harbour a feeling of unkindness against you."

Whilst Mrs. Willoughby spoke, Mostyn continued impatiently pacing up and down the room.

" Then I have lost her," said he, bitterly; " and richly have I deserved to forfeit her regard !—I see she cannot forgive me.—She loves me no longer !—She does not even believe in my unalterable attachment."

" You can hardly be surprised that she should doubt it after what has passed, my dear Captain Mostyn; and, indeed, a little consideration will show you, that under her present circumstances, as well as your own, it is *impossible* she could accept your proposal."

Mostyn made no reply, but appeared absorbed in thought. At length he said,

" I understand what you mean.—It is true!—I do not deserve that Miss Lindsay should trust me, nor can I expect she should put faith in my protestations." An air of deep dejection passed over his countenance. " I will now no longer detain you, Mrs. Willoughby, I can only thank you for your forbearance, for I am conscious I merit all those reproaches from Miss Lindsay's friends which she herself has so generously spared me. And will you assure her—will you assure Miss Lindsay—that the lesson I am now so bitterly learning will not be without profit to my future life. I could say much more—I might beg of you to tell her that—but it is useless!—She would probably refuse to listen to any thing from one who has so deservedly forfeited her esteem.—Still do not let her think too hardly of me, Mrs. Willoughby; and when ——" He seemed desirous, though unable, to say more; and taking Mrs. Willoughby's hand, and warmly pressing it, hastened from the room.

CHAPTER V.

To-morrow came. The carriage at the
appointed hour drove up to the door,
and nothing remained to be done but the
last melancholy ceremony of leave-taking.
Leave-takings are always melancholy pieces
of business, even when it is to return to
a happy home, and friends still dearer than
those one is parting from. To Adelaide it

was peculiarly so. She looked back upon the bright happiness of the last few weeks, and the future looked blank and dreary, indeed, in comparison. Alas! from that happiness what had she reaped? The bitter experience which ages more than years; for without it, a man, should he live to a hundred, to all intents and purposes is still a child; while knowledge of the world makes men of boys. The last few hours had changed the joyous-hearted, confiding girl into the thoughtful, serious, feeling woman.

Frederick and his little sisters were in despair when they found they must lose the kind and sympathizing sharer in all their little joys and sorrows; the gay and amusing companion of all their pleasant rambles and excursions. Mrs. Willoughby, it is needless to say, shared their sorrow. Miss Hawkstone was fortunately on a visit to some friends in the neighbourhood, whom she had joined by appointment at the ball, and had not returned to Bury Hill; and was thus spared the crime of a malicious triumph, the occasion for which, had she been present, she would neither have been slow to perceive, nor to take advantage of.

It is unnecessary to accompany Adelaide upon her journey. Her thoughts were so absorbed, her spirits so depressed, that she would scarcely have paid attention to any occurrence on the way, had it been ever so worthy of note. As it was, she met with no more stirring events than usually befall a stage coach traveller, and arrived, with her escort in due time, at G———, and at Mrs. Melton's door.

That worthy lady greeted her with her usual volubility, and was full of all the little trifles which had occurred during her grand-daughter's absence, and of inquiries about her visit, though Adelaide had con- stantly written to her, relating every thing that she thought would interest her. This must now, however, be all repeated; but as Adelaide had avoided making any par- ticular mention of Captain Mostyn in her letters, she was spared any questions con- cerning him. She exerted herself to enter- tain the good old lady to the best of her power, however painful to herself; for it may easily be imagined she felt little inclined to the recapitulation of scenes and events,

every particular of which could only probe
and lacerate the wounds from which she .
was suffering.

The next morning's post brought a letter
from Mr. Brown, to say that he would join
her the following day, and accompany her
on the next to Lady Kynnaston's, who was
anxious that she should come to her as soon
as possible.

Adelaide was rejoiced that her duties
would begin so soon, for she felt that exertion would be her best auxiliary in overcoming recollections which she wished to
banish for ever from her mind ; and which,
while she was unoccupied, could not but
recur with all their painfully depressing
influence. She felt it her duty to forget,
yet her affection for Mostyn would sometimes

revive with startling intensity; and she would regret the bar she had herself placed against their union, and doubtingly ask herself if the sacrifice had been so absolutely necessary? Then she would be overwhelmed with self-reproach at her weakness; or would writhe under an almost intolerable feeling of shame and degradation, as the particulars of their last interview recurred again and again to her memory.

Had Mrs. Willoughby been still with her, to point out to her, that in her conduct there had been nothing reprehensible, and that all her sensations were natural and innocent, she would have suffered much less; but such consolation must be at hand, must be perpetually repeated to administer relief to feelings such as Adelaide's—feelings which were becoming almost morbid from preying upon themselves; for there was no one now to whom she could open her thoughts, or from whom she could obtain advice and sympathy.

Mr. Brown, upon his arrival, was struck with the alteration in his ward's appearance. She had lost her brilliant colour, and that air of life and animation which gave so much character to her expression. She evidently exerted herself to appear as usual, and her grandmother had perceived no difference; but the more discerning eyes of Mr. Brown observed with pain the abstraction which seemed to carry her far away from the present, whenever any pause occurred in the conversation, or the start with which she would return to the subject of discourse, when her attention was claimed by some question or remark.

In the evening, after Mrs. Melton had gone to rest, he inquired of her, with much solicitude, if she was well? and whether she felt equal to the task which lay before her?

Adelaide assured him that there was nothing amiss with her, and that, far from being alarmed, she was looking forward to " beginning life," as she called it, with much curiosity and pleasure ; and as she seemed indisposed to dwell upon the subject, he made no further allusion to her appearance, and concluded that her low spirits proceeded from the very natural regret she must have felt at leaving all her kind friends at Bury Hill.

CHAPTER VI.

AT six o'clock the next morning, our travellers started upon their journey. It was before these rapid railway days—by the way, what becomes of all the time that they save ?—and when a coach, with four horses, took two days to make the journey from G—— to Portsmouth.

To those who travel for the sake of travelling—travelling, alas! has now lost nearly all its charms. Where are the delightful inns, where one enjoyed all the freedom and comforts of home, and all the excitement and novelty of a visit? Where the civil, curtseying landlady, the bustling chambermaid, and prompt and ready waiter? Where the supper-teas, with their poached eggs and potted meats, their fresh breads and buttered toast, the hissing urn and allowances of black and green tea? The passing steps, the ringing bells, the rattling of coach and chaise under the hospitable arch—the merry chat by the side of the cheery fire, as one buried oneself in an arm-chair, or stretched at full length upon the sofa, while the youngest or freshest of the party concocted the fragrant beverage?

Where the comfortable bed-rooms and downy bed, in which a pleasant fatigue ensured refreshing sleep, in spite of the never-ceasing noise and clatter? Where are they all?

Poor Adelaide, however, made none of of these reflections. We seldom value what we do not expect to lose, nor was she much disposed to enjoy any thing.

From Portsmouth, they crossed to Ryde, in the neighbourhood of which Lady Kynnaston was living. An hour's drive, brought them to the spot. It was a pretty house, of moderate dimensions, surrounded by a verandah, and close to the sea, which, when the tide was up, washed the low wall which bounded the flower-garden.

Lady Kynnaston received them with

quiet courtesy, her manners were too distant to be called kind. She appeared to
be about thirty. Her features were very
beautiful, but so pale, and so still, that they
looked as if they were sculptured in marble.
It seemed as if the heart to which they
belonged must lie dead and cold within her
breast, to give an expression of such deso-
late rigidity to the countenance. Adelaide
felt that some melancholy history must be
attached to that face, a history which would
probably die unrevealed with its possessor,
who appeared as incapable of requiring, as
of bestowing sympathy. About her whole
appearance was an air of the simplest, yet
most dignified refinement, which reminded
one of an Ionic column, and which exercised an imposing fascination, if such an

epithet may be used, upon all who approached her.

"I should wish to introduce your pupils' to you, if you are not too tired with your long journey, Miss Lindsay," said Lady Kynnaston, when the first civilities and common-places had passed between her and her guests; and, ringing the bell, she told the servant to desire the children would come in.

Two little girls soon made their appearance. The youngest, who appeared to be about six years old, was a pretty engaging little thing, rosy cheeked, and golden haired; she ran at once into the room, and to her mother; but the eldest, a pale, delicate-looking, and plain child, some two years older, lingered at the door, and seemed too shy to come forward, till her mother spoke.

"Come here, Clara," said she, in a still, cold voice; "do not stand in that way at the door. I wish to introduce you to this lady."

The little girl coloured slightly, and with eyes bent upon the floor, timidly approached her mother.

" This is Miss Lindsay, the young lady who will in future be so good as to teach you, and I trust she will find you *both*," with an emphasis upon the last word, which, from her again heightening colour, the eldest seemed well to understand, "good and docile children."

"Oh, mamma! we will be very good, won't we, Clara?" cried the youngest.

Clara made no reply; her eyes were still bent upon the carpet.

"Well, then," said Lady Kynnaston, "go up and shake hands" with Miss Lindsay;" and as she spoke she stroked the child's flaxen curls, and kissed her forehead.

Adelaide observed that at the dress Clara cast a glance, quick as lightning, upon her mother, and then her eyes again sought the floor; she did not, however, make the slightest move to follow her sister's example, who, in obedience to her mother's desire, went to Adelaide, and put up her rosy mouth to be kissed.

"Clara! did you hear me? Go to Miss Lindsay!"

The child did not stir, but her face grew

crimson. Lady Kynnaston repeated her command, but in a voice rather cold than stern. Still Clara made no attempt to obey.

"Then leave the room," said her mother, in a voice so chilling that it seemed to come straight from the North Pole.

Clara hesitated a moment, and then crept silently away; she was soon followed by Thekla.

"I fear that you will find one of your pupils most difficult to manage, Miss Lindsay," began Lady Kynnaston. "Clara is obstinate, or dull, or both. I cannot understand her. I find it quite useless to be severe with her; indeed I have tried all means to overcome her surprising stubbornness, but without effect. But her sister is very different—as different in disposition as in appearance."

"She does, indeed, seem very shy," said Adelaide.

"I fear you will find that the least of her defects," said the mother.

There was something about Clara, which interested Adelaide deeply, notwithstanding all that Lady Kynnaston said in her disfavour. She could not avoid suspecting that some unhappy mismanagement or misunderstanding lay at the bottom, and felt eager to penetrate the little girl's apparently impenetrable character.

Lady Kynnaston pressed Mr. Brown to stay as many days as he could spare; but he was too much occupied to avail himself of her invitation, and accordingly returned to Cambridge the following day.

Adelaide lost no time in commencing her new duties. With Lady Kynnaston's able assistance, she arranged a plan of studies for her little pupils, and soon became deeply interested in her employment. Thekla, a frank, affectionate little thing, with quick abilities, and lively spirits, gave her little trouble; and, in the course of a few days, was as good friends with her, as if she had known her all her life; but Clara gave her more trouble.

The first few days, she would hardly speak. She would learn her lessons with apparently the greatest assiduity; but when she came up to repeat them, she seemed to have entirely forgotten them, and had to be

"turned down," as the school-room phrase
is, over and over again.

Lady Kynnaston was, at first, a good
deal in the room, and if she happened to
be present at the time, it was worse than
ever. The little girl, with her eyes bent
upon the floor, remained impenetrably silent.
She seemed as if under a spell. Entreaties,
remonstrances, threats, all were without
avail; till her mother, in that chilling voice
so peculiarly her own, would order her to
leave the room. Then the tears would
gather to her eyes, and she would
slowly retreat to the nursery. Lady
Kynnaston was convinced that it was
obstinacy.

"I passed the door of the nursery, this
very morning," said she, "and Clara was

repeating her lesson, that very lesson of which now she will not say a word, to the nurserymaid, and finished it without a mistake. What is to be done with her? She gets worse and worse."

"She is nervous, I feel sure," said Adelaide. "I am sure she is frightened."

"Hardly, I should think, Miss Lindsay. I do not know what in her own mother there should be to alarm her. Thekla does not think me so very terrible! But I observe that the moment I come into the room, Clara goes into one of her fits of obstinacy, or alarm, as you more indulgently term it, and no power can make her speak."

Adelaide could say no more; she could only hope when left to herself, that she

might be more successful in her manage-
ment.

As soon as Lady Kynnaston left the room,
Adelaide went up stairs to the nursery. The
servants had gone down to dinner, and Clara
was there alone. She was sitting on a stool;
a little dog was in her lap, the unfortunate
lesson book on a chair before her, and, as
she repeated her task to herself in a low
voice, tear after tear fell upon the head of
her favourite, which she kept gently stroking,
whilst he would every now and then look
up with an inquiring eye into her face,
as if he were asking her what was the
matter.

Adelaide remained watching the child
unobserved for a few moments, and then,
advancing, said—

" Well, dear, is that lesson learnt at last?"
in a cheerful encouraging voice.

Clara remained perfectly silent.

" Come, my dear, speak !"

Not a word.

" Now, Clara," said Adelaide, stroking
her head, "you pain me, and are giving me
a great deal of trouble. It is a lovely day,
and I want to go out. Have you learnt
your lesson ?"

" I *do* know it,—but I can't say it."

" Oh, yes, you can if you try. It will
please your mamma if you will say it to
me."

Clara handed Adelaide the book, and
began in so low a voice, that it was almost
impossible to hear. However, she repeated
it very correctly.

"Now," said Adelaide, when it was finished, "put on your bonnet, and come with me into the garden—your mamma and Thekla are there; and your mamma will be very much pleased when she finds how good you have been at last." She was most anxious that Clara should not imagine that she thought Lady Kynnaston unjust. An expression of joy passed over the poor child's pale countenance; she quickly fetched her bonnet, and, taking Adelaide's hand, went with her into the garden.

Lady Kynnaston was sitting on the lawn, while Thekla was playing with some shells at her feet; on a little table at her side, stood a basket of peaches.

As they approached, Clara's courage seemed again to fail, and she hung back a little; but Adelaide urged her forward, and said to her mother,

"I am sure you will be glad to hear, madam, that Clara has said her lesson, at last, and very perfectly."

Clara cast an imploring look at her mother, while the colour flew to her face.

"Has she?" said Lady Kynnaston in her icy tone. "I am glad to hear it ; but I should have been better pleased had she said it whilst I was in the room. Such obstinacy I cannot excuse! But, as you have said your lesson at last, here is a peach for you, Clara ;" and she took one from the basket and offered it to her daughter.

It was painful to watch the changing expression in the poor child's face during this speech. At the close it changed from

despair into impenetrability; and the prof-
fered fruit fell from her hand upon the
grass.

Lady Kynnaston rose with an offended
air. "I see you have not recovered your
temper, Clara," said she. "Do not stay
here, you disturb me."

Clara did not move. She seemed fixed
to the earth.

"I do not wish to have the annoyance of
another argument with you, I am fatigued
enough with the first; and if you do not
choose to obey me, I shall, myself, go into the
house;" and she turned away.

Clara's lips moved, and she made an
effort to catch her mother's dress as she
passed; but she missed it, and again remained motionless.

"Come, Miss Lindsay," said Lady·Kynnaston, "you must be quite tired with your day's exertions. I beg you will take no further trouble about Clara.—Pray come!" she repeated in a tone almost of command, as· Adelaide·lingered.

There was no help for it, Adelaide was obliged to follow; though she was filled with compassion for the poor child's evident suffering, and longed to endeavour to make her peace with her mother.

"You see how it is," said Lady Kynnaston, as they walked together towards the house, "obstinacy the most determined, or, perhaps, still worse, pride the most ungovernable!—I am in despair, Miss Lindsay, and know not what to do with her!"

"Perhaps, sympathy," began Adelaide.

"I can have none, with such a temper," said the mother; and, indeed, the contrast was so striking between the commanding figure and noble features of Lady Kynnaston, and the shrinking, timid, air and pale, thin face of the little girl, that Adelaide could not but believe her. "No openness; no confidence;" continued Lady Kynnaston, " nothing but that impenetrable silence, and tears. If she would fly into a passion; I could understand it; but that silence!—I confess it irritates me."

"Indeed, madam, I feel persuaded it is extreme susceptibility. Clara is, evidently, a very timid child. I am afraid you will think me forward in venturing my opinion, inexperienced as I am; but, I think, that with gentle encouragement, Clara would become all you wish."

"I find no difficulty with her sister, Miss Lindsay. *She* does not appear to find me so terrible; but *she* loves me, and Clara does not." As she spoke they arrived at the house, where Lady Kynnaston was met by a servant, who handed her a note, which required an immediate answer. She went up to her sitting-room for the purpose, and Adelaide could not resist returning to the lawn to see what her little pupils were about.

They were no longer where she had left them; but after a little search she thought she heard voices proceeding from a small shrubbery. She entered it, and had not made many steps down a narrow, winding path,

when she saw the two children seated at
the root of a tree, a little further on, and
with their backs towards her. She approached without being overheard.   Little
Thekla had her arm round her sister's waist,
who was weeping as children only can weep,
silently; but with such a flow of tears, that,
like Undine, she seemed as if she would
weep herself into a fountain ; so hopelessly,
so disconsolately, that Adelaide felt almost
inclined to follow her example.

Thekla was urging, entreating her to
speak, and seemed to have just succeeded in
prevailing upon her, when Adelaide came up.

"Oh, Thekla," sobbed she, "I want my
own papa! I want him to kiss me. Mamma
won't kiss me—I did not want the peach.
—Oh, papa! papa !"

"I will run and ask mamma to kiss you," cried little Thekla. "Come, Clara," pulling her by the hand, "do come; she will do it directly when I ask her!" and again she tried to pull her sister from the ground.

"No, Thekla, I can't come—I can't speak—and then mamma is angry."

"That is just it," cried the little one, "you never will speak; and you used to talk so to papa, and that vexes mamma.— Why don't you talk to her as I do?"

"Oh, I cannot!" sobbed poor Clara; and there was another flood of tears.

Thekla jumped up, ran down the path, and was out of sight before Clara could recover her voice sufficiently to call after her.

Adelaide now came forward.

"Clara, dear," she began, "you must not cry in this way; it will make you quite ill; and then what will your papa and mamma say?"

"Do you know papa?" exclaimed the little girl, her tears suddenly stopping, while she looked eagerly in her governess's face.

"No, I do not—but what will he say when he comes home, and finds his little girl has not been good, but has foolishly cried herself quite ill?"

"He is not coming home!" said the child, sadly. "I shall never see him again—I hoped he would have come, but he never has!"

This was the first time Adelaide had ever heard the father's name mentioned. She had supposed him to be dead; but now, from what the child had just said, she imagined herself to have been mistaken, for Clara was quite old enough to understand what was death, and the impossibility of seeing her father again,—was he no longer in life ? Some mystery seemed attached to him ; but she felt a natural delicacy in endeavouring to obtain a knowledge from the child which the mother had not thought proper to impart ; so she said,

" He will come home some day, I dare say; and then he will be sorry to hear that his little Clara, from her behaviour, has given her mamma reason to think her obstinate and ill-humoured. You should try, dear, to *make* yourself answer your mother when she speaks to you. It is very tiresome when a little girl will give no reply, but remains as silent as if she were dumb—who can say whether her thoughts are not proud and rebellious ?"

Adelaide continued her little sermon in gently soothing accents—the little girl's confidence seemed quite won, and she promised to try and conquer her timidity. She seemed yearning for a love and affection, which, from some cause which to Adelaide was inexplicable, she had evidently never met with from her mother, though they were lavished upon Thekla. Thekla, it was true, was lovely, engaging, and open-hearted; whilst poor Clara was plain, somewhat awkward, and of rather slow parts. But surely, thought Adelaide, such adventitious claims should not exercise so exclusive a charm upon a mother's heart, however they might affect the world in general.

"Come home now, my dear," said she, when the little conversation was ended, "it is nearly tea time, and your mamma will be waiting."

They walked hand in hand to the door, Clara chatting cheerfully away till they reached the hall-door. Tea was already laid out when they entered the drawing-room; Lady Kynnaston was sitting upon the sofa; Thekla, kneeling upon a low stool at her feet, was reading to her from a story-book, which her little fat arms was supporting upon her mother's knee.

"Now, mamma!" cried she, as her sister and Adelaide entered.

"Come here, Clara," said Lady Kynnas-

ton ; " Thekla has begged me to kiss you,'
and she pressed her lips upon the child's
forehead, who timidly approached her.
" Why do you look so frightened ?"

" I am not frightened, dear mamma,"
said Clara.

" Very well, my dear—I hope you are
sorry for your behaviour to-day, and that
you will endeavour in future, for your own
credit's sake, to conduct yourself more
agreeably."

Ah ! thought Adelaide, would she but
have said " for my sake," or " because it is
right to do so."—"*For her own credit's
sake!*"—What child, generous and single-
hearted, would be influenced by such a
motive ?

Clara evidently struggled violently with

her disinclination, and compelled herself to say that she would try and be very good.

"You are a good girl *at last*," said Lady Kynnaston.

Even this cold enconium seemed to gratify the poor child beyond measure. Her countenance beamed with happiness, and she knelt down by Thekla's side at her mother's feet, as if she would read with her. Unfortunately, she knelt upon her mother's dress, rather awkwardly, certainly, and dragged it from the waist.

"Get up!" said Lady Kynnaston, quickly, "you are upon my dress, Clara!"

Clara rose instantly, with a fallen countenance; she lingered a little while by her mother's side, and then walked away to the bow window. Adelaide felt for her.

"Mamma!" said Thekla, "call Clara back!"

"I did not send her away, my love; she can come if she chooses," was the reply; "go on with your reading."

The little girl obeyed, but seemed restless and uncomfortable.

Adelaide in the meanwhile made tea, and when she had poured it out, called to Clara to come and take it, who, upon the summons, crept forward with that timid, scared air which seemed so irritating to her, mother, who glanced at her, as she passed, with an expression half of impatience, half dislike, but took no further notice of her; and Thekla, having finished her reading, entered into conversation with Adelaide. Conversation was a gift which Lady Kynnaston possessed in a remarkable degree. Her opinions were original and clever, her information most extensive, her mind highly cultivated. Adelaide greatly enjoyed her company; she could not but remark, however, that any approach to the inner life, to feelings and affections, seemed studiously avoided by Lady Kynnaston; and if Adelaide happened in any way to touch upon such subjects, she was met with the most chilling reserve, or a kind of sceptical indifference which precluded any advance.

The little girls, in the meanwhile, were amusing themselves with some game or other at the table. Thekla was often very noisy; but her laughter and exclamations passed unnoticed by her mother, except when at some lively sally she would now and then give her a fond smile; but Adelaide could not but observe that whenever Clara raised her voice above a whisper she was immediately silenced. There arose some little dispute about the rules of this game. To any impartial observer it was evident which of the sisters was in the right, and Adelaide anxiously awaited Lady Kynnaston's decision, to which Thekla triumphantly appealed.

"You are quite wrong, Thekla," was the answer; "Clara is undoubtedly in the right, and you must abide by the rules of the game."

A flush of joy again kindled in Clara's countenance, and the game was resumed.

Adelaide felt relieved. Lady Kynnaston was then too high-minded to indulge herself in positive injustice. All might still be well.

The nurse now came to fetch the two children to bed. Clara got up immediately and went to say good night to her mother, who, engaged in conversation, gave her an inattentive kiss ; but when Thekla came up and threw her arms around her, she embraced her almost passionately. Clara stood by, and seemed to count the caresses which were bestowed upon her more fortunate sister. She then turned away, after Adelaide had affectionately bidden her good night, and went to her nurse. As usual, that night, she cried herself to sleep.

Numerous were the little scenes of a
similar nature to which Adelaide was a
pained, though deeply interested, spectator.
She almost despaired, at times, of Clara
ever obtaining her mother's affection.   The
poor child was always so constrained in her
manner to her mother, so evidently ill at
ease in her presence, that she never did
herself justice ; whilst Thekla's remarkable
beauty, and engaging and affectionate
manners, contrasted in a manner most
unfavourable to her sister.   Thekla
was very demonstrative, and though a
generous-hearted little thing, probably
showed more feeling than she possessed ;
Clara, timid and reserved, felt far more
than she showed.   It was the same in their
studies.   Thekla, quick and giddy, learnt

very rapidly, and forgot as soon; Clara, rather slow and very reflective, learnt with difficulty, but what she once understood, she retained.

This difficulty of apprehension annoyed and irritated her mother; she mistook slowness for stupidity, and reserve and timidity for obstinacy, and could, as she declared, do nothing with her; but under Adelaide's patient and gentle instruction the child's mind seemed gradually to develope, and Adelaide was surprised at her progress.

In matters of positive fact, Lady Kynnaston was never unjust. Clara, also, enjoyed all the little prerogatives belonging to seniority, and had ever the first choice and the first turn. With these concessions to justice Lady Kynnaston's conscience seemed perfectly satisfied, and provided she discharged them with strict impartiality, seemed to consider her affection as of right, at her own disposal, and that she was free to lavish as much upon one child as she thought it impossible to bestow upon the other.

Lady Kynnaston had never made the slightest allusion to her husband, though Adelaide had now been several weeks in the house. If it had not been from the mention made of him now and then by the little girls, she could never have supposed him in existence ; but from what occasionally dropped from them she found no reason to alter the opinion she had already formed, and felt convinced that he was living; though what could occasion this separation from his family she could not possibly conjecture.

K

CHAPTER VII.

ONE day Adelaide and her little pupils set off for a long walk, accompanied by the nurserymaid and a donkey, upon which the children rode in turns. Adelaide had heard of the beauties of Priory Bay, and had a great wish to visit it.

They went by the sands, the tide being out sufficiently to allow of their passing;

and in about an hour they reached Sea-
View, then a small village, inhabited only
by pilots and fishermen. Adelaide here left
the children in charge of the nurserymaid
to eat the luncheon they had brought with
them, and walked on to the Bay alone, as
they were tired, and preferred resting. She
was enchanted with the beauty of the scene.
The sea lay calm and unruffled, dotted here
and there by the sail of a distant fishing-
boat, and bounded by the rich and diver-
sified country on the other side of the
channel; while behind her, the banks were
broken with rocks and clothed with trees
and underwood, which, when the tide was
in, feathered down to the very edge of the
water.

She opened her sketch-book and began to

draw; but while her pencil almost mechanically traced upon the paper the scene
which lay before her, her thoughts travelled
far away; to Bury Hill, to the last time
that she had opened that sketch-book—the
last time she had seen Captain Mostyn—the
day of the scene in the arbour. She had
never had the courage to open it since; and
now the past rose to her memory, softened,
it is true, by the time which had elapsed,
but still most painful. Mostyn came before
her in all the fascination of his manner,
with all his dangerous tenderness; but he
had lost her esteem, and she felt that she
loved him no longer. It was her own pure
and high imagination which had clothed
him with qualities he did not possess.—
The idol had fallen from the pedestal upon

which she had enthroned it, and now lay in fragments at its foot.

Still the experience she had endured was not without its influence upon her mind; that spring-like freshness, which had once been so distinguishing a feature in her disposition, seemed faded and saddened, and her character had taken a deeper tinge. She felt older, wiser, graver than before; her sympathies, if possible, more enlarged; her benevolence more extended; her selfishness, — she never had much — still diminished. Suffering had purified and exalted her character, as it ever does those that are the noblest. The "precious balms" had not "broken her head."

She heard constantly from Mrs. Willoughby, and one of her last letters had

informed her that Captain Mostyn had gone
abroad with his company. This was the
first and only mention which her friend had
ever made of him; and Adelaide, though at
first she could not overcome a longing
almost intense, to see even his name mentioned in her letters, could not but acknow-
ledge to herself that her friend exercised a
wise discretion in refraining from, even in
any way, alluding to him. She was not
aware that there was another reason besides
the consideration of *her* happiness which
made Mrs. Willoughby so desirous that
Mostyn's memory should fade from her
heart.

Absorbed in such thoughts, Adelaide had
not observed that the sky was becoming over-
cast. Dark clouds threw their shadow upon

the waters, and the sea-gulls floated scream-
ing over head; every thing betokened an
approaching storm; and when Adelaide,
whose attention was at last accidentally
aroused, looked at her watch, she found to
her dismay, that she had been sitting drawing
more than two hours. She hastily gathered
her things together, and walked rapidly to
the spot where she had left the children.
They were in no hurry to be gone, for they
had been as much engrossed with their
sand-castles as Adelaide had been with her
reflections, and entreated that they might
be allowed to wait till the tide, which was
gradually rising, should fill the moats which
they had dug around them.

Adelaide pointed to the sky, and told
them it was impossible; besides, the

very tide which, if they waited, would fill their mimic trenches, would prevent them from reaching home by the shore, and it was a long way round by land.

Thekla was very obstreperous, and declared she would stay; and then, finding remonstrance was useless, escaped from her nurse, who in vain attempted to hold her, and shrieking with laughter, ran off as fast as her little fat legs could carry her, in the opposite direction from home. There was a chase in pursuit, and the nurse brought back the little rebel, now in floods of passionate tears. It was useless attempting to pacify her, so she was lifted on the donkey, and they at length proceeded on their way home; Adelaide first ascertaining from an old fisherman who was standing near, that there was no danger of their being cut off by the tide.

All this took up a good deal of time. The rain began to fall ere they were half-way home, and before they reached it descended in torrents. The whole party was completely drenched.

Lady Kynnaston had been out in the carriage, and had only returned home five minutes before the arrival of Adelaide and her children. She was on the point of sending a servant with umbrellas to meet them, when they made their appearance.

She was too polite to make any reproaches to Adelaide, for an accident such as this; but ordered a fire immediately in the nursery, where the children were quickly undressed, and put into a warm bed. She showed more anxiety than from her apparently cold and impassible nature would have been supposed possible; but all her solicitude was for Thekla. Though the bed of the eldest child was first warmed—though she was first helped to the hot tea which was prepared for them and Adelaide, yet Thekla was undressed by her mother's own hands, and Clara was consigned to those of the nurse. Clara was left to amuse herself; but lady Kynnaston sat down by Thekla's bed-side, showed pictures and related stories to her.

Clara observed them for some little while in silence; at length she timidly asked her mother to sit a little nearer to her, that she also might hear her. Thekla had fast hold of lady Kynnaston's hand, and exclaimed, at her sister's request :—

"No, no, dear mamma, you mustn't go! I like to hold your hand!—You can read to yourself, Clara."

"But I like to hear mamma tell stories best, Thekla, and if mamma will sit there I can hear her as well as you."

"No, no," repeated the little thing, half in fun, "she shan't go, I tell you.—Darling mamma! stay with me. I like to have you by me, so much, so much!" and she kissed and caressed her mother with winning fondness.

"You are quite old enough to amuse yourself, Clara," said lady Kynnaston.

"Sarah!" to the nursery-maid, "give Miss Kynnaston a book."

Clara took it, without another word, and pretended to read ; but tears silently flowed from her eyes, and so blinded them, that had she been inclined, she could not really see a letter.

" Mamma," said Thekla, presently, " Clara is crying. Please go and sit where she asked you."

Her mother turned round, and looked towards the other little bed.

" What are you crying for, Clara ?" inquired she, coldly.

No answer.

" When will you learn to conquer this childish weakness ? " continued her mother. " Tears, tears, at the slightest contradiction ! You are too old to indulge in such behaviour !"

Sobs now shook the poor child's bed.

"Really, Clara! this is too bad. I cannot sit down by your sister, but you are offended; and at the slightest reproof you lose your temper."

"Oh, mamma! mamma!—indeed I am not cross," sobbed Clara.

"I am glad to hear it, Clara. I should hardly have supposed so from what I have witnessed," in the same cold voice; "prove it to me, by restraining your tears."

But this appeared out of the little girl's power. She was tired with her long walk, wounded by the fresh manifestations of her mother's preference for her sister, every mark of which she had been watching with the jealous eye of unrequited affection; and her tears, instead of being checked, flowed faster than ever, while her sobs were re-doubled.

"I cannot stand this, Thekla," said lady Kynnaston. "If Clara chooses to be so childish, she cannot expect that I will remain a witness of her behaviour. In half an hour you may come down—Clara can remain in the nursery;" and she rose and left the room, passing Clara's bed, without a look or another word.

"Don't cry so, Miss Clara," said the old nurse, who, seated at work, had been a witness of the whole scene. "Never mind, dear! you will bring on one of your bad head-aches."

Little Thekla jumped up, ran across the floor, and getting into her sister's bed, endeavoured to comfort her with the most affectionate caresses ; but it was of no use, Clara's tears still fell in torrents.

" Come, come," said Mrs. Morland, " this will never do! I will fetch Miss Lindsay."

Adelaide, fatigued with the day's excursion, was lying down in her dressing-room, when Mrs. Morland knocked at her room-door and entered.

" Pray, Miss Lindsay, come up stairs to the nursery—that poor child is crying ready to break her heart!"

" Who, Clara ? Is she hurt ?"

" Not as you mean, Miss, but in a manner far worse. It is the old story—her mamma is displeased with her ; though what for," continued she, half to herself, " it would puzzle one to know."

" Pray, Mrs. Morland, fasten my dress,"

said Adelaide, " and I will go to her immediately."

"Just as it was with Sir Thomas," continued the old woman, in the same tone,
hooking the dress as she spoke, " I don't
mean any disrespect to my lady, Miss, but
no temper on earth could stand that way
she has—Sir Thomas bore it a long time,
but every thing must come to an end, and so
did his patience.—Lor! I have hooked up
your dress all wrong, Miss! I must begin
it all over again—I knew how it would be
all along," continued she, " when people
can't marry those they like——"

"Pray," said Adelaide, interrupting
her, " hand me that ribbon." She felt
she had no right to the information
the old nurse was evidently burning to

give, relative to her mistress's former history.

But Mrs. Morland would neither take the hint, nor let her go.

"Stop, Miss," said she, "let me settle your collar;" and then continued, while Adelaide was fastening the buttons of her sleeves,—

"My Lady never took to Miss Clara; whether it was because Sir Thomas always seemed to love her the best of the children, or whether he loved her best because she made so much of Miss Thekla, I can't say. However, she never seemed to care for her eldest, and Miss Clara has found that out long ago, poor child!—Ah! it's a sad pity! But as I was saying, when people marry a person they don't much care about, still, if that person is kind and loving to them, they may very likely get to love them very much in their turn, and all turn out happy; but if people marry one they don't care about, all the time loving another, no good *can* come of it, take my word for it, Miss Lindsay!"

"I am quite ready to go to the nursery, now, Mrs. Morland," said Adelaide, moving towards the door; "shall we go?"

"If you please, Miss.—I don't know how it is, but no one but you can ever quiet Miss Clara, when once she gets into her crying fits—poor, dear child!"

They went into the nursery—Clara was still weeping, while Thekla in vain endeavoured to make her cease or speak.

Adelaide went up to the bed.

"Now, dear Clara, we must have no more crying!—you are tired with your long walk, poor child; we must not take another if it . fatigues you so much. I am come to tell you and Thekla a story, and then you must go to sleep."

She began her relation immediately; and gradually as the child got interested, her sobs ceased, and her tears dried up, and by the time the story was ended, Clara, quite worn out, fell into a sound slumber.

Adelaide was most anxious that the child should not . imagine for a moment, that she herself perceived the occasion of her grief. She knew that nothing could be so dangerous in this instance as open sympathy; and she always carefully avoided giving Clara the slightest reason to suppose that she was in any way aware of Lady Kynnaston's partiality.

Thekla had, in the mean time, gone down to the drawing-room; but Adelaide remained sitting by the sleeping child, in whose thin pale hand her own was fast locked, and she could not withdraw it without awakening her. Her thoughts reverted to what Mrs. Morland had just been saying. Some mystery then there evidently hung about the family, or if not a mystery, at least,—some history. Lady Kynnaston, with all her faults, interested her deeply. She always gave her the idea of some fine instrument out of tune; as if some adverse fate had rendered those tones discordant, which nature had formed for producing the finest harmony. Was there then no means of restoring the jarring notes? Adelaide could not but hope so, though it seemed a work beyond the power of mortal to effect.

Adelaide longed to win her love; to penetrate that heart, which she felt sure glowed warm beneath the ashes of a blighted affection; for, from what had dropped from the old nurse, she felt persuaded that this was at the bottom of Lady Kynnaston's history; and well could she sympathise with her in her sufferings. Ah! if she would but open her heart to her, her sympathy might do her good. The sympathy of the young is so consoling; but she despaired of ever obtaining more than Lady Kynnaston's approbation, for she seemed as incapable of returning affection as she seemed indifferent to inspiring it. "Besides," thought

Adelaide, " I am but a stranger to her: what does she know of me ? how am I entitled to hope for confidence ?   Ah, had she but a sister! some near relation to show her, but with kindness and sympathy for the sufferings she has no doubt undergone, how far, far she is astray ; how ill she is per- forming her most obvious duties! then from her high mind and strict conscientiousness, one might yet hope for the happiest results."

CHAPTER VIII.

" WHAT a clever sketch, Miss Lindsay!" said Lady Kynnaston, one afternoon, as coming into the school-room, she stopped to look over Adelaide's shoulder, who was drawing, " I was not aware that you were such a proficient in the art."

" I am very fond of drawing," said Adelaide; " If you care for such things, perhaps it would amuse you to look over this portfolio," and she handed her one that lay beside her.

" Thank you," said Lady Kynnaston, " I shall like it very much ; but do not let me disturb you ; pray go on with your work." She opened the portfolio and turned over the drawings in silence, beginning at the latter end, which was full of views of the Isle of Wight and of the neighbourhood of Bury Hill. Adelaide in the meanwhile continued painting in silence.

She was suddenly interrupted by an exclamation from Lady Kynnaston.

" The.Falls ! Jamaica !—How came you by this sketch, Miss Lindsay ?" asked she.

" Simply from its being one of my own handy-works," replied Adelaide, smiling ;

" but I do not consider it one of the best things I have ever done.—I think I have improved since then.—The colouring is too gaudy, and must strike an European eye as unnatural; but it is really not in the least exaggerated. I am sorry you did not begin at the other end of the portfolio, that you might have seen the best the last," added she, with all the *amour propre* of an artist.

" It is not as a work of art that I am considering it," said Lady Kynnaston. " But you say it is your own doing,—have you ever been in Jamaica then ? and do you know the Falls ?"

" Do I know the Falls !" exclaimed Adelaide ;—" the happiest time of my life has been spent there !"

" Can it be possible !" continued Lady

Kynnaston,—" Tell me, Miss Lindsay, can you have been any relation to the late Mr. Lindsay, of the Falls?"

" I was his only daughter," said Adelaide, in much surprise at Lady Kynnaston's manner.—" Pray tell me in your turn, why it should be a matter of so much interest to you.—You could hardly have known my father; he must have left England long before you were grown up, and I never heard him mention your name."

" I have never seen him; nor did I ever know any thing of him personally," said Lady Kynnaston.—" We were such very distant connexions; besides, you know, no communication was ever kept up between the families."

" But you have not told me, Lady

Kynnaston," cried Adelaide eagerly, " what families! — how are we connected ?"

" My father stood next in succession to Mr. Lindsay, failing heirs male," replied Lady Kynnaston, " and at Mr. Lindsay's death, the estate of the Falls reverted to us : and, as you probably know, my father has resided there ever since he came into possession."

"Are you then a daughter of Mr. Harrison ?" exclaimed Adelaide, almost breathless with surprise.

" Exactly so," said Lady Kynneston.

Adelaide rose,—they both remained silent for a few moments.

" And so then,—" said Adelaide, breaking the pause.

" So then," interrupted Lady Kynnaston,
" we are relations ; and most happy am I,
dear Adelaide," embracing her, " to claim
you as such.——But how strange that we
should so long have remained 'in ignorance
of our mutual connexion."

" You have never asked me any questions
about my former history," said Adelaide,
" and I was not likely to volunteer the information. Nor in Lady Kynnaston was I
likely to recognise a Miss Harrison ; but I
am surprised that my name, coupled with
the little you *did* know about me, never
struck you."

" It was strange certainly, and I am surprised also that I did not discover this before ; but you know we were perfectly
ignorant of each other's families.——Our

fathers have never even met; and though mine stood next in succession to the property, yet Mr. Lindsay was so young a man when he left England a widower, and considering the circumstances, it was so natural, were it only for the sake of his daughter, that he should wish to leave a *son* in possession of the estate, that every one believed the reports which were continually reaching England, of his being about to form another connexion; and it was not till long after my marriage, that my father began to think it probable that the Falls would revert to him. And now," continued she, " I can hardly tell you, how glad I am that some fortunate chance has brought you into my family. I do not know how it was, but I always felt a regard for you beyond

what I generally bestow upon strangers.
My family is all abroad; besides," added
she, bitterly, " if they were at home, I
could not make friends of them.—I want a
friend.—Ah, Adelaide! you little know how
much——." She stopped, her eyes glis-
tened with moisture, and her voice trembled;
but before Adelaide could reply, Lady Kynnaston, as if ashamed of the emotion she
had so unusually betrayed, drew herself
up, struggled for one instant, and then
recovered the cold composure so habitual
to her.

Adelaide was greatly disappointed. She
had longed to tell her, how she had only
waited for the permission to love her—how
she also longed for a friend! But now all
expression of her feelings seemed impos-

sible. That chill barrier of *manner* was again raised between them—that magic barrier which it seemed impossible to surmount.

At her request, Adelaide related to Lady Kynnaston the particulars of her father's ruin and death, to which she listened with great interest. At the close of her narration, Lady Kynnaston again embraced her, and as the tears fell from Adelaide's eyes at the recollection of the fatal event which had deprived her at once of both her father and her home, she said,—

"Poor child! You have begun life and its sorrows early! But to possess such a father as your's, though only in memory, is far, far more enviable than the actuality of fortune and parents such as . . . . . such as

some are blest with.   Believe me, your trials
are slight indeed compared to those of
many !"

She then asked where she had been, and
what she had been doing since her return to
England.

Adelaide gave her a brief account of her
grandmother—of Mrs. Willoughby, and of
her visit to Bury Hill; of course avoiding
all mention of Captain Mostyn.

" There seems another connecting link
between us," said Lady Kynnaston, when
she again concluded, " The Mr. Latimer you
have mentioned, I am well acquainted with."

" Ah! now you mention it," replied Adelaide, " I remember Mrs. Willoughby having
told me something to that effect.—Is he not
guardian to your children ?"

"Hardly, in their father's life-time. But he is Clara's godfather, and Sir Thomas Kynnaston's oldest friend."

"He is a most excellent person," said Adelaide. "I liked him so very much, and he was very good-natured to me. He was almost my first acquaintance in England, as I have told you."

"I expect him here, shortly, on his return from abroad. He came to see me before he went, the end of July last. I was shocked to see him looking so ill and out of spirits; he never mentioned having met you at Bury Hill, which I am surprised at, as he told me that he had been staying there for a few weeks in the early part of the vacation. Did he know that you were coming here?"

"He could not have been aware of it

then, as I did not hear of you till some time after his departure," answered Adelaide.

"I cannot account for his never having mentioned your name," repeated Lady Kynnaston. "He could hardly have been ignorant of the connection between us, that is to say, if you ever mentioned to him any thing about The Falls."

"I am sure I must have done so in the course of conversation, even if he had not heard my history from his sister, which is of course almost impossible. But you say he was Sir Thomas's friend; perhaps he knew little of your own family—as little as I did myself—and possibly the identity of *my* Falls with *your* father's estate in Jamaica never occurred to him."

"Possibly; more particularly as your name is by no means an uncommon one. But still it is strange that he never mentioned having seen you. I should have thought," added Lady Kynnaston, smiling, "that the fact of having made *your* acquaintance, Adelaide, would hardly have passed unnoticed in conversation with an intimate friend."

"I must say it is not very flattering to me," said Adelaide, "and I confess, I was vain enough to imagine that Mr. Latimer was so kind as to like me, a *little* bit; for we saw a good deal of each other at first. Afterwards," said she, blushing, "I don't know how it was exactly—but there were a great many parties—and people staying in the house—and I did not see so much of him—I think he was very busy reading and writing. I know he was engaged in some difficult Greek translation, and I believe it was upon that account that he left Bury Hill much sooner than he had at first intended. I remember attributing his paleness and gravity to this same deep book upon which he was engaged."

"Very probably," said Lady Kynnaston. "I know that he attributed the illness under which he was evidently suffering when I saw him last, to hard study, and was going abroad for change of air and scene."

There was a few moments silence, during which both the ladies seemed lost in thought. At last Adelaide ventured to say,

"You said that Mr. Latimer was coming

to see you soon. Do you expect Sir Thomas to accompany him?"

"I do not think he can come," was the reply.

"Is Sir Thomas abroad?" continued Adelaide, urged on, in spite of her discretion, by an irresistible impulse.

"I believe so—I don't know," said Lady Kynnaston, searching for a shade of lilac from amongst the heap of wools which she turned out of a bag upon her lap.

"How glad he will be to see you and the children again!" said Adelaide.

Lady Kynnaston's face flushed crimson.

"How provoking!" exclaimed she, rising suddenly, the wools falling about her feet a mass of tangled confusion; "I cannot find

this shade! I must have left it up stairs;"
and she left the room.

Adelaide felt vexed with herself for what
she had said; as Lady Kynnaston was certainly annoyed. She perceived, with disappointment, that whatever confidence her
cousin might obtain from her, she, evidently,
was to expect none in return; and yet she
now longed more than ever, from real interest, not idle curiosity, to fathom the mystery which lay at the bottom of Lady Kynnaston's history—to know what it was that
occasioned the obvious estrangement between
her and her husband, and to whose fault it
ought to be attributed.

She feared that from what she had seen
of Lady Kynnaston, and what little she had
casually heard of Sir Thomas, the blame

must be mainly attached to the wife. But faults, no doubt, there must be upon both sides. The discovery that had just been made of her connexion with Lady Kynnaston, gave her much pleasure. Say what they will, there is a tie in kindred.

Adelaide had now, as it were, a right to the affection she had longed for, and a right to her interest in Lady Kynnaston's happiness. Then, too, she was now no longer a stranger; and she intuitively felt, that little as Lady Kynnaston's manner expressed it, she too felt the influence of relationship, and looked upon Adelaide in a far different light than before. It also gave her pleasure to think, that she should have an opportunity of renewing her acquaintance with Mr. Latimer, an acquaintance which

she so much valued; in short, she closed
her eyes that night with a feeling of happiness to which she had long been unaccus-
tomed.

CHAPTER IX.

WINTER was now fast approaching. The autumn, which had been unusually fine, had passed pleasantly by; the daily tasks varied by many pleasant excursions about the beautiful island. Furnished with drawing materials, books, and a basket of provisions, our little party would set off early in the open carriage, drive to some picturesque spot, and spend the whole day out of doors.

Lady Kynnaston showed daily increasing affection for Adelaide; but though there occurred fewer of those painful scenes between her and her eldest child, it was more to be attributed to the improvement, if it can be called so, in poor little Clara's manner, than to any greater degree of kindness on the part of the mother. Thanks to Adelaide's gentle remonstrances, and kind and sensible method of treatment, she was gradually overcoming that nervous timidity of manner which seemed so irritating to her mother. Instead of maintaining an impenetrable silence, she would now answer with cheerful alacrity, or respectful excuse, when her mother addressed or found fault with her, which last was still far too often the case.

Perhaps her mother's coldness was at length reaping the fruits it might have been expected to produce, and that the child, more indifferent to an affection, which, if such a feeling can be attributed to one so young, she despaired of obtaining, was less pained by the manifest preference which was shown to her sister. However that might be, she seemed to take refuge in Adelaide's love, and to wish for nothing more when in her society. Never from the very first had she shown the least jealousy of Thekla. She loved her too dearly to harbour such a sentiment; and indeed the generous and ardent affection which that loving and engaging little being, unspoilt in this particular, ever showed to her sister, rendered such a feeling utterly impossible. This bitter poison was not infused, then, into her disposition, but no thanks to Lady Kynnaston.

It was one evening, about the end of November, that Mrs. Morland came up to Adelaide's room, in a great fuss.

" Pray, Miss Lindsay," said she, " go to my lady, and try to prevent her going out; Mrs. Nash, that poor bed-ridden woman, to whom my lady is so kind, has sent to beg that she will send her some medicine for her youngest boy who is very ill. She says she has sent for the doctor, but he is gone to Cowes, and she thinks her child will die before he comes back. I know there is fever in the village, and I am afraid of my life, lest my lady should catch it in those low places. But she says, how can she send medicine without knowing what is the matter? and so she is putting on her things, and going directly.—Pray, Miss, don't let her!"

Adelaide went immediately to Lady Kynnaston's room, who she found putting on her shawl.

" Mrs. Morland is very uneasy at your going out this evening, Lady Kynnaston," said she ; " and, indeed, with your delicate chest, it is very imprudent. Do let me go and see the poor boy instead. I will bring you an exact report of the case."

" Indeed, Adelaide, you shall do no such thing," replied Lady Kynnaston. " It is some idea of a fever that nurse has got

into her head, which alarms her—not that I
shall catch cold—I believe it is all nonsense on her part, for I have heard nothing
about it."

"But Mrs. Morland assures me that there
is fever in the village," urged Adelaide;
"and it is such a risk to run! I have not
the least fear of infection—do let me go
instead."

"I am not going to expose you to a
danger—if danger there is, which I do not
believe—that I avoid myself, my dear."

"Oh! dearest Lady Kynnaston, let me
entreat you——"

"Say no more about it, Adelaide, I have
made up my mind upon the subject," interrupted Lady Kynnaston, in a tone which
quite put a stop to further objections; and

drawing on her gloves, she went down stairs, and Adelaide heard the hall-door close after her, as she left the house.

In half an hour she returned.

"I am very glad I went," she said. "The poor child is suffering very much; and I have sent him a cooling medicine, which I hope will do him good. He has a dreadful sore throat, and a great deal of fever."

"Scarlet fever!" said Mrs. Morland, in that particular tone, which expresses as plainly as the words themselves, "I told you so."

"Oh nonsense! nurse," exclaimed Lady, Kynnaston. "You always make the worst of things! I tell you it is a very bad sore throat."

"Scarlet fever, my lady, for all that," persisted the old woman.

"Oh, well, have your own way, Mrs. Morland.   I know by experience it is of no use arguing the point with you.   Scarlet fever be it then, so that you do not insist upon my having taken it."

"I suppose, my lady, you will not think proper to have the children down to tea to-night, nor to go up yourself to the nursery?" said Mrs. Morland, more in the tone of an assertion than of an interrogation.

"Oh! if you choose me to perform quarantine, I suppose I must submit," replied her mistress; "but I think you are rather absurd, Mrs. Morland."

"Perhaps it is wiser to be upon the safe

side," interposed Adelaide. "The doctor will no doubt be able, when he sees the case, to decide whether there is any reason for alarm—and you would never forgive yourself were it to prove scarlet-fever, and the children were to take the infection."

"I should think that their own mother is not likely to be indifferent about their wel-fare, Miss Lindsay," said Lady Kynnaston, rather haughtily, "and as I made no objection to Mrs. Morland's excessive prudence, it is hardly necessary for you to throw your weight into the scale. Advice in this instance is undesired and unrequired."

Adelaide said no more, but turned to the table, and proceeded to make tea. She knew by experience that it was useless to attempt either defence, explanation, or remonstrance in such cases as these; and as she filled the tea-pot from the urn, she fell into one of her frequent musings over the strange inconsistencies of Lady Kynnaston's character; and could not but confess to herself how insupportable must be such a temper to a husband.

The next day the Doctor called to say that the boy had undoubtedly the scarlet fever, and of a most virulent description; he strongly advised that the children should not approach their mother till it was decided whether she was herself free from the infection. The evening of the next day, Lady Kynnaston looked flushed and ill; but she would not allow that any thing was the matter with her; declared it was only the effect of the fire, which, as she had felt very chilly, she had been sitting too near; and though her hands were burning, persisted that they were just comfortably warm; nor would she hear of a physician being called in.

However, the next morning she could not deny that she had a violent head-ache, and that her throat was very sore; still she maintained that she had only a bad cold, and that she had often felt the same symptoms before. Towards the evening she got rapidly worse, and no longer objected to allow Dr. Fenwick to be sent for.

He arrived about nine o'clock, pronounced Lady Kynnaston's illness to be scarlet fever, and recommended that the children should be sent from home. Lady Kynnaston was very anxious that Adelaide should go with them and Mrs. Morland, lest she also should take this terrible disorder; but Adelaide would not hear of it; and, accordingly, the nurse went alone with the children to the hotel at Ryde, early the following morning, whilst Adelaide remained to tend their mother.

Lady Kynnaston's illness was most severe, and at one time her life was despaired of. Adelaide hardly left her night or day; and to her unremitting care, under Providence, might be attributed the patient's ultimate recovery. Doctor Fenwick was delighted with her conduct, with her watchfulness, presence of mind, and good sense; and declared that many lives might be saved could the physician's orders be always seconded with so much zeal, and executed with such precision and punctuality, as was displayed in this instance.

In the crisis of her illness, Lady Kynnaston was very delirious, and then, when all bars and locks seemed opened, and the deepest secrets of her heart were poured forth, exaggerated, and uncontrolled, Adelaide alone remained by her bed-side, and with eyes moist with pity, was an unwilling listener to the affecting and incoherent exclamations which poured from the sufferer's lips. One name was perpetually repeated; now in tones of tender endearment, now in passionate exculpation, now invoked with heart-rending distress. It was a name which Adelaide had never heard before; and, though Lady Kynnaston's father and mother would be addressed in her ravings, sometimes with the most pathetic entreaty, and again in· remonstrances amounting sometimes to defiance, yet that of her husband was never uttered.

One night, after a very severe attack of the delirium above described, Lady Kynnaston fell into a deep slumber. Dr. Fenwick told Adelaide that the ultimate termination of the disease would be decided by the state in which she would awaken from this heavy sleep; and Adelaide watched through the hours of night with indescribable anxiety, listening to the heavy breathings of the patient, and dreading every moment that she would break forth in a fresh paroxysm of delirium.

It was about six o'clock in the morning, and Adelaide was employed at the hearth, endeavouring noiselessly to supply the fire with a little fresh fuel, when she heard her name gently called from the bed.

" Adelaide, is that you?"

" Yes, dearest Lady Kynnaston," she answered, hastening to the bed-side, and perceiving with delight the languid composure of her patient's manner.

" I feel as if I had awakened from a frightful dream.—I have been very ill, have I not?—Where is Thekla?—where are the children?"

" They are quite well; but they are not here. Do not you remember?"

" Ah, yes; they were sent away from the house.—I have had the scarlet fever, have I not?"

" Yes, you have, and most severely; but

thank Heaven, you are out of danger," replied Adelaide, fervently.

"Have I been dangerously ill, then? and have you been with me all the time? My dear Adelaide!—The last few hours have seemed to me like a dream; but all through I have had a vague consciousness of your being near me. Were you not afraid of the infection?"

"Oh, no!" replied Adelaide, "not in the least. I did not take it at school when many of my companions were ill with it."

"How can I ever express my sense of your tender kindness, dearest Adelaide!" exclaimed Lady Kynnasten.

"Say no more now, dear Lady Kynnaston," interrupted Adelaide; "you must be very quiet;" and she laid her hand upon that of her friend.

Lady Kynnaston closed her eyes, and remained silent for some little time; at length she said,—

" How long is it since I was taken ill ?"

" Six days ago."

" Indeed! so long?—I had no idea of it." She was again silent.

" You say I have been dangerously ill," she once more began, " but I have no recollection of great suffering."

" You were happily unconscious at the crisis of the malady," replied Adelaide. " But, indeed, Lady Kynnaston, you must not talk."

There was another pause, which Lady Kynnaston was again the first to break.

" Fever ! " said she,—" Unconscious !—
I had a fever several years ago ; and they
told me, when I recovered——." She
stopped, and then continued in a low voice,
which she in vain attempted to render
indifferent, while she averted her eyes
from Adelaide's face,—" Have I been de-
lirions ? "

" Indeed, Lady Kynnaston, if you will
not be silent, I really must leave the room.
Dr. Fenwick left the strictest orders that
you should be kept quiet. When you are
better you may ask me as many questions
as you like. And now take this draught,
and afterwards you shall have some tea.
I daresay you are very thirsty."

Lady Kynnaston swallowed the medicine
which Adelaide poured out for her, and

soon after fell again asleep. Her quiet and regular respirations, made a delightful contrast to the painful slumbers Adelaide had previously so anxiously watched, and which appeared to afford no rest to the sufferer; and with joyful gratitude, she felt that her friend was no longer in danger, and impatiently awaited Dr. Fenwick's arrival, that he might confirm her hopes.

About twelve o'clock, she heard his carriage drive up to the door, and she stole from the room to meet him, and to give him an account of his patient's state.

"She is saved!" he said, when Adelaide had ended. "I feared, at one time, I confess, that she would have sunk under the disorder. I shall not go to her now, for fear I should disturb her, and I cannot leave her under better hands than your's, Miss Lindsay." Then, after a few more general directions as to the treatment to be pursued, he took his leave.

Adelaide returned to the sick room, and, in obedience to the Doctor's commands, maintained the greatest quiet ; indeed, Lady Kynnaston appeared languid and exhausted, and seemed herself little to desire conversation.

CHAPTER X.

LADY KYNNASTON'S recovery was surprisingly rapid, and in a few days she was allowed to sit up. It was then that, seated in an arm-chair by the fire, she spoke again of her illness; and, after thanking Adelaide in terms most gratefully affectionate, for the tender care she had shown her all through, again approached the subject of her delirium, though with evident repugnance.

"You did not answer me *one* question I made you the other morning, dear Adelaide," said she. "I wish you to tell me,— was I delirious?"

"You were very much so, in the height of the fever," replied Adelaide.

"I have heard," continued Lady Kynnaston, "that delirium, like intoxication, is a revealer of secrets.—Tell me," with an attempt at a laugh, "what did I disclose?"

"Nothing that I could make much of, dear Lady Kynnaston. You addressed many people, and seemed very unhappy," replied Adelaide.

"Many people!" repeated her friend.

" Can you remember any of the names?
It would amuse me to hear what, or whom
I raved about."

" You̅ spoke of your father and mother,"
answered Adelaide.

" And of whom else?"

" Some one whom you called Max."

Lady Kynnaston sank back upon the
chair; a deep blush overspread her countenance.

" After so many years!" exclaimed she,
" Is it possible?—Come close to me, Adelaide dear, your kind, your more than sis-
terly devotion, deserves a sister's confidence.
—Listen to me, and I will tell you my
story. I daresay it may often have per-
plexed you."

" Adelaide seated herself on a stool at

her feet; her hand was clasped in Lady Kynnaston's, who thus began.

"I need not relate to you my birth, parentage, and education, further than to say that I was one of a large family, that my parents were straitened in their circumstances, and that as we grew up they found it impossible to educate us, as they wished, in England. I was the eldest of their children; and when I was about fourteen, they determined to take us abroad, to give us those accomplishments which they wished us to possess. I must tell you, my dear, without affectation, that I was very handsome;" Adelaide looked up in her beautiful face, and thought such information was hardly necessary, "and that my parents were quite bent upon my making a 'capital match,' and to obtain this object of their desires, I was to be furnished with every means of captivation that accomplishments could give me. I was not particularly dull, and made sufficient progress to satisfy them. They were very proud of my appearance and of my proficiency in music, languages, and all the etceteras.

"My brothers, in the mean while, were growing up, and getting rather beyond school-room discipline. It became necessary to put them under higher authority than that of Mlle. Schwartz, our governess; and my father was beginning to consider what plan he should adopt with them, when he became acquainted with Maximilian von L——, a young man of a noble house, but whose family had been utterly ruined at the time of the last war. He was recommended to my father as a person of first-rate ability; and as he had not succeeded in obtaining the Diplomatic situation for which he had applied, and to which his family misfortunes and great talents well entitled him, it was thought that he would not refuse to occupy himself with instruction, till he obtained an appointment more dignified and worthy of him.

"My father accordingly made him a proposal, which was accepted, and he came to instruct my brothers for three or four hours every day. He soon acquired their respect, and they made rapid progress under his tuition, while both my parents became, apparently, quite attached to him, and were always pressing him to spend the evening at our house.

"I was now nearly eighteen. We went very little into society, and Maximilian was the only person we were really intimate with. If we had been intimate with hundreds, it would have been the same! I would have chosen him amongst them all!"

Lady Kynnaston stopped for a few moments, and then proceeded.

"I need not dwell much upon this part of my life, Adelaide. We were thrown constantly together, and what might have been expected, took place—we became attached to each other. How well I remember the evening when first I discovered that our affection was mutual!

"Maximilian, with his usual frankness

and straightforwardness, went the very next
morning to my father, and asked for m
hand. My father would not hear of it !
such a match was far below his expectation
for his daughter; he was astonished at Vo
L——'s presumption! and even hinted
with contempt, at his situation as a tutor.

" Maximilian quietly reminded him that i
there *was* question of a *mésalliance*, i
would not be upon the Harrison side ; an
said that he was as well aware of the foll
of marrying without the means of main
taining a family as my father coul
be; that he did not expect my fathe
would give his consent to an immediat
union; and that he only requested permis
sion to continue his addresses to me, unti
he should succeed to the appointment whic

he had been promised, and which would certainly be vacant in a year or two; as the present incumbent would be promoted upon the death or superannuation of the old man who occupied the post above him.

"My father would not, however, listen to him. Maximilian flew to my mother; but she was equally obdurate; and all she would do for him was to consent to his seeing me once more.

"It is now ten years since that meeting, that parting rather, dearest Adelaide! But every word, every look is still fresh upon my recollection! I told him that I would never forget him, and I have kept my promise—but not, fool that I was, as I intended him to understand it! On his part, he declared that, would I but be faithful to him, some time we would still be united; that he felt that within him which assured him of his advancement, and that he would yet place a coronet upon my brows.

"My father sent for me as soon as Maximilian had left the house, and tried at first gently, and, as he found I would not give way, at last with violence, to make me promise I would think no more of 'that adventurer!' as he contemptuously styled the man whom, but the evening before, he prophesied would be, one day, prime minister. But I had a spirit as determined as his own, and declared that nothing should ever make me forget him, and that I would speak to him whenever we might chance to meet. At last my father gave up the useless contest, and I flattered myself that so far, at least, I had come off victorious ; but my father was more of a tactician than I had given him credit for.

"About ten days after this, my father received a letter from his sister, who had married a man who had made a large fortune in trade, and whose daughters were rather older than myself, inviting me to come and pay them a long visit. I had not seen any thing of my cousins since we left England, and on every account was extremely disinclined to accept it; but it was useless objecting. I am convinced that my father, seeing how firmly I was attached to Maximilian, and considering that change of scene and the allurements of society would be the best means to effect a cure, had written to my aunt asking her to invite me. It was not likely that my remonstrances would induce him to alter his plans.

"He accordingly brought me himself to England; and after spending a few days at Belmont Place, the name of Mr. Smith's large, staring house in ——shire, returned to the Continent. I think we hardly exchanged one word from the time of our departure from W—— to his return there!

"My cousins, the Miss Smiths—you must not think me very ill-natured, Adelaide—were plain, vulgar, and ill-educated, and endowed with all the insolent envy of *parvenues*. They had nothing to be proud of but their wealth, so they took special care to concentrate all of the ingredient which they possessed, and I assure you there was no lack of it, upon that one advantage. They were mortified beyond measure when they discovered that 'the poor cousin' possessed talents and external advantages which all their father's money could not procure for themselves—and though I was not of a nature to resign myself quietly a victim to their ill-breeding, still they had it in their power to mortify me in numberless ways, and I should have been unhappy even if there had been no other cause than their behaviour to occasion it. You may, then, easily imagine how wretched I felt!—separated completely from Maximilian—without a possibility of even by chance hearing how he was going on, or, what he was doing! and with the additional pain of considering that most

probably he also was in utter ignorance of
what had become of me, since we had
left W—— in such a hurry that no report,
even of where I had been removed, could
have reached him.

"I wrote repeatedly to my mother,
urging her to allow me to return home,
and even promising that I would not see
Maximilian till my father should consent to
our union. But it was in vain! And at
last I received a letter from my father, so
insulting, that dignity, pride, call it what
you will, prevented me from ever alluding
to the subject again.

"My cousins lived in a continual round
of gaiety, balls and parties almost every
night; people were constantly staying in
the house; and they could not conceal their

vexation at the attentions I invariably met with.

"I had been at Belmont Place about six months, when some excitement was created in our circle, particularly amongst the young ladies, by the report that Sir Thomas Kynnaston, a wealthy young baronet—need I say that he was unmarried—was come to live at his fine place in the neighbourhood. It had been shut up for some time; as the old Sir Thomas, his father, hated the country, and resided constantly at Leamington. Now his father was dead, and the son had determined to open the old Hall once more.

"Every house in the neighbourhood of any consideration left cards at the Hall. Endless parties were made for its master,

and everywhere he was to be met with.
You may be sure that my cousins would
not allow my aunt to be behind-hand in
the race; and he was a constant guest at
Belmont. I could not be so blind as not
to perceive *who* was the attraction; nor
were my aunt and cousins less penetrating,
if penetration it required to discover what
was so very evident.

"And now, Adelaide, I am coming to the
sad part of my story. Even now I cannot
think of it without anguish, or forgive
those who so foolishly, so wickedly deceived
me!—But they, perhaps, did not contemplate the misery they would occasion. They
did evil that good, as they thought, might
come; and bitter have been the fruits."

Lady Kynnaston's manner grew excited,

her cheek flushed, and her hand became burning hot. These symptoms did not escape Adelaide; who, in the midst of the interest she had felt in the narrative, had been disturbed by fears that the excitement would be too much for the convalescent. She now took advantage of the pause, and begged Lady Kynnaston to defer the remainder of her history till the next day, on account of her health.

Lady Kynnaston consented; and soon after retiring to her bed, Adelaide left her for the night.

Her thoughts naturally reverted to what she had just heard. She could not but feel shocked at the manner in which her cousin had mentioned her parents; and felt that no treatment on their part could absolve a

child from filial respect and duty. Lady
Kynnaston's moral education had evidently
been most defective. No attention appeared
to have been paid to the formation of her
character, however much might have been
expended upon the cultivation of her talents,
she evidently considered the misconduct of
others as quite sufficient *reason* for her own;
as for *excuse* she seemed never for one
moment to suppose it required.

CHAPTER XI.

THE next day Lady Kynnaston resumed her history.

"I told you, my dear, that I was coming to the sad part of my story; and now I am led to suppositions to explain what followed, though I feel morally convinced that my conjectures are true. Sir Thomas, as I said, he showed me very plainly, though I must say, most unobtrusively, that all he required to make his intentions still more unmistakable, was a little encouragement on my part. That encouragement, you may well believe, I was little inclined to give. To my surprise, however, my cousins began to urge me to do so, though at first they had seemed so jealous of any preference which he showed for me. I can only account for this by supposing, that as they at last despaired of making a conquest on their own account, they wished to get rid for ever of a dangerons rival, and, at least, stand *cousins* to the hall, since there was no chance of any of them being installed as mistress.

"I should have told you, that, from many an occasional taunt, I had discovered long before, that my cousins were aware of my attachment to Maximilian ; of course they derived the information—no doubt with many an interesting particular—from my parents ; but be that as it may, they began at this time to attack me more openly ; and even my aunt would urge upon me the necessity of overcoming what she styled 'so foolish a *penchant*,' and of the duty that I was under to establish myself 'well in life;' and free my parents from any further anxiety about my welfare. But I remained as firm as a rock, and treated what I considered as so unwarrantable an interference with the indifference it deserved. I was determined, if called upon, to act a firmer part than Lucy Ashton, and to yield to no persecutions or persuasions. I little

thought, in my pride, that I should do pre-
cisely the same, and fall a victim to a like
deception!

"I am certain from what followed, that
my aunt or my cousin Eliza wrote to tell
my parents of the excellent match it lay in
my power to make, and of my obstinacy in
declining to encourage its offer. No doubt
they added, that nothing but my 'idiotic'
preference for another could account for my
indifference to Sir Thomas; for I received,
about this time, a letter from my mother in
which was the following sentence, written
just at the end, and as if the intelligence it
conveyed were a matter of no moment to
myself or to any one else. I remember the
words as if they were now before me.

"'Oh, I forgot to mention amongst my

other gossip, that young L——, that clever young man, who you may remember used to instruct your brothers, has received an excellent appointment; thanks, it is said, to his interest in the affections of the fair daughter of the Herr Kammerrath Von P——. You may recollect her, a very pretty girl with a quantity of flaxen hair, that he used to talk so much about. However, to whosoever interest he may be indebted for his appointment, it is certain—at least I have it from the best authority—that they are engaged, and shortly to be married.'

"Adelaide, I cannot describe to you the effect these words produced upon me!—I never for one moment doubted their truth; for I well remembered the young lady, with whose brothers Maximilian was very inti-

P 2

mate, and many were the jealous pangs which his avowed admiration of her beauty had occasioned me, before I was assured of his affection for myself. I knew, too, that her father possessed powerful patronage, and I did *not* know how low a woman, and that my mother, could stoop to deceive!

"A more gentle nature than I am gifted with, would probably have melted into tears, have drooped, perhaps died. But I kindled into indignation and burned for revenge. My imagination ascribed all sorts of thoughts to the heart of Maximilian. I saw now how it was!—He considered our attachment as a school-room episode, the sooner forgotten the better!—If he had really cared for me, he would have contrived to find out where I was!—He would have written !—He would have found some means to assure me of his continued attachment !—Fool that I was, to be so deceived !—And then, Adelaide, I remember, I started up, and walked about the room in a perfect frenzy. I never considered how inconsistent with the noble and straightforward character of Maximilian would have been any secret correspondence unsanctioned by my parents.

"As soon as the first paroxysm of my agony and indignation abated, I began to consider how I should conceal the wounds from which I smarted. I felt sure that the letter for my aunt which had arrived enclosed within my own, would convey to her the same intelligence, and I could not endure the thought that my cousins should

discover the suffering which Maximilian's
desertion occasioned me—that they should
taunt me with being forsaken!—jilted!—
wearing the willow!—I writhed at the very
idea! and thought that any thing would
be more endurable than their insulting compassion.

" I accordingly determined to give the
letter to them to read with apparent un-
concern, to affect complete indifference, and
finally, as a proof of it, to receive with
favour the attentions of Sir Thomas.

" In pursuance of the course of action
which I had laid down for myself, I went to
my aunt's *boudoir*. She was sitting there
with my cousins, and they were all talking
together when I opened the door. Upon
my entrance they immediately ceased. My

aunt held her letter open in her hand. I am confident that both she and my cousins fully believed the account it contained. They were, it is due to them to say, as much deceived in this respect as I was myself.

"I walked up to her with a steadiness and self-command which even now surprises me, saying,—

"'Perhaps, aunt Smith, you would like to read mamma's letter to me. There is a great deal about the new house into which they have moved.'

"I gave her the letter, requesting that she would send it me back when she had read it, and then left the room, humming an air. In about a quarter of an hour Eliza returned it me.

" 'Poor Geraldine!' said she, in a tone of mocking compassion. 'It's a long way to send a *basket* all the way to England, isn't it?—As it's made of *willow* it won't be very heavy to carry, that's one comfort.'

" I suppose she meant some allusion to a *korb*, which you know is also in German a refusal of marriage; but though I could not very clearly see the appositeness of her remark, she seemed delighted with her awkward pun herself, and went away laughing.—How could I be so great a fool as to mind the ridicule of such creatures as these!

" Well, Adelaide, Sir Thomas came the next day, and I treated him far differently than I had ever done before.—I talked to him, listened to him, smiled at him; in

short, gave him every encouragement. He
seemed enchanted; and so it went on for
some days, till one night at a ball, he took
courage to make me an offer of his hand, in
a manner so frank, and so devoted—so
humble, and yet so manly, that it must have
gone straight to the heart of any other
woman. For myself, I only felt exultation
that I was revenged upon Maximilian; that
if he had cast me off for a counsellor's
daughter, I was not behind him in the race,
but would show him that I also could forget
in favour of a Baronet's son; and so I at
once accepted Sir Thomas, felt proud of his
advantages of exterior and fortune, and longed
that Maximilian could see how well I bore
his loss, and how admirably his place had
been supplied. Of course Sir Thomas

wrote the next day to my father to ask his consent, offering the most liberal settlements.

"My father's consent, you may be sure, was not long in arriving; nor did I make any objection to a speedy termination, by marriage, to our engagement. I had made up my mind to this result, and cared not how soon it took place. I longed for the intelligence to reach Maximilian. Every thing I thought, every thing I did, bore reference to him.—And yet I fancied that I hated him!

"I can hardly describe my feelings towards Sir Thomas. I do not think I had any, without it was annoyance at his expressions of affection. I am surprised that he was not disgusted with my coldness. Perhaps he had been so accustomed to flattery—to being "run after," that conduct so much the reverse, interested him.

"Our wedding was fixed for the first Thursday in the ensuing month, and my father and mother came over to attend it. They were, of course, enchanted with the match, the advantages of which fully equalled their expectations for me. Not a word, you may well believe, was ever said of Maximilian."

"Did you never say any thing of your previous attachment, to Sir Thomas?" asked Adelaide, with some little surprise.

"Not a word!" replied Lady Kynnaston. "I dare say, you, in your honourable uprightness, in my place would have done so —but my education, Adelaide, has been

different from your's.—It would have been,
as you may easily believe, very painful, very
disagreeable to me to do so ; and as it was
disagreeable, I never thought of alluding to
the subject. With him I was not upon
those terms of intimate confidence, which
the deepest affection can alone inspire. I
never talked to him about myself. I
thought I did my duty sufficiently by pre-
tending to listen to all he said to me of
himself, while my own thoughts were meanwhile, perhaps, engaged in drawing com-
parisons between his conversation and
that of Maximilian. How different !—Sir
Thomas was a very sensible man, but his
mind was uncultivated, though his *head*
was remarkably well-informed. He never
thought. Maximilian was made of thought.

Sir Thomas read the "Times."—Maximilian adored Shakspeare. In short, my dear, to use a metaphysical phrase, Maximilian's mind was *subjective*, that of Sir Thomas *objective*; but his disposition, I must in justice say, was as faultless as Von L——'s.

"At length, to my great satisfaction, the wedding-day arrived! I was tired of the courtship—I was tired with the never-ending fuss about dresses · and trimmings, plate and jewels.—I longed to say good bye to my aunt Smith and my cousins; and the sight of my father and mother was a perpetual source of irritation to me. When I was once fairly married, I hoped I should think no more about Maximilian, and intended to be very tolerably happy, and enjoy all the pleasures that wealth, independence, and an indulgent husband could bestow.

"Well, Adelaide, we were married.

"I must tell you, that in the hurry and excitement, the letters which the postman brought as usual that morning, had been unopened by any of the party to whom they might be addressed. My mother, amongst others, had received one, which she put aside till her return from church. It was from one of my sisters. After the breakfast, she went up stairs with me, and while I was changing my dress for the journey, she suddenly remembered this letter, and drew it from her pocket to read. 'There would be no doubt,' she said, 'many affectionate messages and congratulations for me to receive before my departure.'

"'Oh!' cried she, 'there is a letter enclosed for yourself from one of the girls ;— but they have all got to write so like Mdlle. Scwartz, that I am sure I can't tell from which of them it is.—I will put it in your bag, Geraldine—it will amuse you on your journey.'

"'The carriage is at the door, Geraldine!' cried one of my cousins, rushing in ; 'and Sir Thomas is asking for you.'

"'My dear!—make haste!' said my mother. 'You must not keep Sir Thomas waiting ;' and she jumped up as she spoke, and her letter fell to the ground.

"I quietly proceeded with my dressing, for I saw no reason for all this hurry, and at length went down stairs. Morland, who had formerly been my nurse, and who had accompanied my mother from Germany to be present at my wedding, and whom I had begged might be allowed to enter my service—Morland was already seated with the servant behind ; I bade my adieu to all my relations, and was handed by Sir Thomas into the carriage.

CHAPTER XII.

"It was at Loch Katrine, one rainy after-noon, about four days after the wedding ; Sir Thomas was out fishing, and I felt very dull and out of spirits, with no book that I cared to read, and nothing to do but watch the rain-drops coursing one another down the window-frames.—Suddenly I recollected the letter which lay still unopened in my bag ;

I drew it out, and throwing myself upon the sofa, broke the seal with a yawn.

"The letter was not from one of my sisters. It was from Max!—Oh, Adelaide! such a letter!—

"It began by saying that, 'having returned to W—— from Russia, where he had been sent as *attaché* to some diplomatic mission, a post which he had obtained through the kind interest of the Kammerath, von P., he had heard of some reports concerning himself, which appeared to have been so industriously circulated, that he feared they must even have reached my ears. To contradict this report, he now addressed me. Nothing but this would have induced him to take a step which, as an infringement of my parent's wishes, he knew I should disapprove.'—

He then went on to assure me of his constancy, of his unalterable affection, in words —Oh, Adelaide! in such words, that I almost fancied I could hear him—could see him speak them!—'He hoped,' he wrote, 'that I knew him too well—that my own affection for him was too firmly grounded, to be affected by such reports—that I could not do him, or myself the injustice to imagine it possible he could forget me.'— The letter ended by saying, 'that he should now very speedily be able to come once more forward, with proposals to which the most *prudent* parents would not object to listen.'

"My heart seemed positively to cease beating as I read! and when I had concluded, I remained seated for a few

moments, without the power to move a
muscle.

" The sound of a footstep upon the stair,
startled me, and my first impulse was to
conceal the letter.   It was not, however, Sir
Thomas—the step passed on, and I breathed
again.   But upon this first impulse I acted.
I determined to leave him in complete ignorance of what had occurred, and to write
one letter—the first and the last—to Maximilian, to tell him of my marriage, and how
miserably I had been deceived.

" I rose to go to my own room for this
purpose, and as I passed the mirror over the
chimney-piece, glanced at my reflection.   I
was as pale as death.   When I reached my
room, I rang the bell, and desired Morland,
who attended my summons, to tell Sir

Thomas, if he should return within the hour, that I felt ill, and should lie down and try to rest ; and requested that he would not disturb me, as I was sure that sleep would alone ease my head-ache.

"'Indeed, my lady,' said Morland, 'you do look ill !—I never saw you such a spectre. —Goodness sake, what ails you ? let me give you some salvolatile.'

"I swallowed the medicine she poured out for me, and then dismissed her, assuring her that nothing ailed me but fatigue.—Of course, I did not lie down, but, bolting the door, immediately began my letter.—What I said I hardly know—I am sure it must have been very incoherent; but the substance acquainted him with my fatal marriage, of the false intelligence which had led me to

the step, and of my bitter repentance
for my credulity. I entreated his forgiveness; and implored him still to look back to
my memory with kindness. It was a
strange, wild, rhapsody; for, indeed, Adelaide, I was almost beside myself. My
forced composure—the restraint I was compelled to put upon any outward manifesta-
tion of my feelings, drove them all within.
I dared not even shed a tear, for fear I
should be questioned by Sir Thomas, and
my brain felt oppressed to madness!

"When the letter was finished, I directed
it, sealed it, and put it in my bag; and then
again rang the bell.

"'Morland,' said I, 'I do not feel better
—I cannot sleep—I am sure the air will
do me good. I shall go out— If Sir

Thomas comes home before I do, tell him that I have gone out walking—I shall be back in half an hour.'

" ' La, my lady!' said Morland, ' it is raining fast! you will get wet to a certainty!—But may be the air will do you good, Miss Geraldine; only don't stay out too long, there's a good young lady.'

" I promised her that I would not, and leaving the inn, walked down the village, and inquired of the first woman I met for the post-office. She directed me to it; and I cannot describe to you the feeling of relief it gave to my mind when I slipped my letter into the box, and saw it vanish from my sight beyond the power of re-call.

" I returned to my room.   Sir Thomas,
to my great satisfaction, was not yet come
back; and now I really laid myself down,
for my temples throbbed as if the veins
would burst, and I had a racking head-
ache.   Thus I remained for another half
hour, in misery indescribable!   I would
have given all I possessed in the world
might I have but been transported for one
single hour to some desert island, where,
unobserved by mortal eye, I might have
given vent to the agony which was pent up
within me.

" There was a knock at the door.

" ' Come in,' I said.

" ' My dearest life!   What is the matter ?'
said Sir Thomas, coming up to my side,
and taking my hand in one of his own, as

he laid the other on my forehead, which was fiery hot.

"I could not endure his touch—his affectionate words stung like scorpions.

"'Don't,' said I, 'your hands are so cold!' and I withdrew my hand from his, and moved my head away.

"'I beg your pardon, my love,' said he, quite gently, 'I forgot I had been fishing all day'—and he continued his anxious inquiries about my health.

"'I wish to be quiet, if you please,' I answered. 'I was just going to sleep when you opened the door—Pray go down stairs again.'

"He left me, but he looked pained. I could not help it. What was his pain in comparison with mine!

"I shall tire you out with my story,
Adelaide," continued Lady Kynnaston, after
a pause; "however, I have little more
to tell you now. Our 'honeymoon' came
to a conclusion, to my great joy; and
we went to Edmonbury Hall, my future
home. It was a magnificent old place,
but I could find no happiness in the
spacious and splendidly-furnished apart-
ments; nor in the beautiful park and
grounds, nor in all the luxuries and
comforts with which I was surrounded.
The attentions I received as Lady Kynnaston, failed even to give me the
satisfaction which they ever administer
to vanity. I was indifferent to my health,
—to my beauty—to my appearance—to
my husband's affection. Perhaps the latter

was the only thing to which I was **not** indifferent!

"Sir Thomas could not fail to perceive my coldness to himself, my failing spirits, and my pale cheek. At first he expressed the greatest anxiety upon my account; and would redouble his endeavours to please and gratify me. But I could not show an affection I did not feel; and at last he seemed wearied out, and his manner, too, grew cold.

"We had no sympathies—no feelings in common. I am afraid I performed my duties as a wife very ill, but it is too late to regret that now.

"Well — Clara was born!— But this event, which to every mother in happier circumstances is one of such tender interest, failed to give me the slightest pleasure. Ah, Adelaide! the child only reminded me of the indissolubility of the tie which bound me to the father!

"Sir Thomas, however, showed the infant a tenderness, which no doubt amply atoned for the indifference of the mother. He seemed to have concentrated all the love which I rejected, upon its head, and spent far more time in the nursery than I did myself.

"Two more years, and Thekla came into the world.

"If you have read Wallenstein, you will know why I begged Sir Thomas would allow me to give her that name."

"Did you regard your second child with

the same feelings that you did your first?" asked Adelaide, pointedly.

"No, I did not," answered Lady Kynnaston; "I loved her from the first. Whether it was that I had become more accustomed to my fate; or whether it was the name—I cannot account for it——and besides, Thekla is so lovely and engaging," added she, " and showed me so much affection.—The other seemed hardly to care for me in comparison with her father.

" Years passed.—The estrangement between Sir Thomas and myself grew wider and wider. He took to politics, and was a great deal in town. He had long ceased to show me those marks of fondness which were repulsed with so much coldness; but still he was as kind as ever, and seemed to forestall my every possible wish. His great friend, Mr. Latimer, was very often at Edmonbury Hall. He did not seem to like me much; but I could not resent what it was so impossible to be surprised at.

"All this time I heard nothing from Maximilian. Of course he never answered my letter; though, will you believe it?—in my secret heart I felt disappointed that he had not. But though I heard nothing from him personally, I could trace his rise in the public prints, step by step, to a post of the highest eminence. His opinions were quoted, his advice governed the destiny of his coun-try; rank, honours, and titles were showered upon his path.—But he never married!— and the belief which I cherished in his con-stancy, kept my own alive.

"One morning in the September of last year, I was sitting at breakfast with Sir Thomas and Mr. Latimer. Sir Thomas always came down for the shooting season to Edmonbury, and Mr. Latimer generally accompanied him.

"Mr. Latimer took up the 'Times,' which lay upon the table, and began reading it to himself.

"Suddenly he exclaimed,

"'Oh, how grieved I am!—what a loss to his country—!What a loss to all Europe!'

"I continued pouring out the coffee in my usual indifferent manner.

"'What's the matter, Latimer?' asked Sir Thomas. 'Who's gone now?'

"'Count L—— is dead,' replied Mr. Latimer.

· " 'Dead!' I cried; and started from my chair as if I had been shot.

· " I never faint, but I stood as if rivetted to the earth without further speech or motion.

"Both the gentlemen rose in alarm.

" ' My dearest Geraldine,' cried my husband, 'What is it?—what is the matter? —Speak, I entreat you!'

" My fortitude gave way. I burst into tears, into sobs which I found it impossible to control, while I called upon the name of Maximilian.—I hardly knew what I said, what I did; but my husband gathered sufficient from my incoherent exclamations to enable him to put interrogations to me, which drew from me the whole truth.—I cared not that he knew it.—I denied nothing.

" ' Why did not you tell me this before ?' said he. 'Have you then deceived me all this time ?'

" 'I never deceived you!' cried I; 'I never feigned an affection I did not feel !—I never wished you to think that I loved you !'

" 'You should have told me this before our marriage,' he said, and rushed from the room.

" Mr. Latimer remained ; and as soon as the violence of my grief was a little abated, addressed me in a kind, but grave and serious manner ; and in terms with which it was impossible to be offended, endeavoured to point out to me how much I had been in error,—how reprehensible had been my conduct towards Sir

Thomas; whilst brooding upon a fate which my own conduct had rendered inevitable,—how selfishly I had neglected the happiness I had promised to cherish; —how slighted a love which I had vowed to return. He urged me now to bury my recollections with the dead; to return to my duties, and endeavour to win back an affection which I had so justly deserved to lose.

" But I could not, I would not, listen to him, Adelaide; though since my illness, in those moments of reflection to which a recovery from a dangerous malady, and the stillness of a sick-room so disposes the mind, I cannot but confess the truth of all he said.

" He was still talking to me when Sir

Thomas returned, and Mr. Latimer left the room.

" I remember there was a quiet dignity in my husband's manner, which even then I could not but notice. He came up to me, but I did not rise; and he remained standing before me, while he thus briefly addressed me.

" ' At last, then, accident has discovered the reason of your conduct! a conduct to me so inexplicable hitherto!—I saw that you did not love me, but I never suspected that you loved another.—I will not dwell upon the pain which your coldness, your want of affection, has given me ever since our marriage; nor will I reproach you with that want of candour, which has occasioned all this misery.—You have deceived me, Geraldine !—You promised that which you were' unable to perform, and concealed from me a fact which had I known——,

" ' I cannot undo the tie which binds us together, but such freedom as I *can* give you, I offer you.—Henceforth we will live separate.—I wish it upon my *own* account. —I can no longer live with a wife whose affections are in the grave of another.' He stopped, for his voice grew thick, and then added, in a tone still trembling with emotion,—' Have you any thing to say ?'

" ' Nothing,' I replied ; ' It is what I wish.'

" He looked at me.—Adelaide, I am afraid I am very hard-hearted.

" ' Mr. Latimer will communicate to me all your wishes,' continued Sir Thomas after a short pause. 'All communication between us will henceforth be carried on through his medium.—All your desires shall be attended to.'

" 'I thank you,' replied I.

" Sir Thomas turned from me, and walked towards the door. On reaching it, he turned back and looked at me once more ; but he saw no sign in me, I suppose, which encouraged him to return, and left the room. He went to London that afternoon, and I have not seen him since.

" My arrangements were speedily made and acceded to by Sir Thomas, who, with great generosity, allowed me to keep his children, that my character in the eyes of the world might be respected. I believe he would have taken Clara, but it was found impossible to separate the children.

" And now, Adelaide, I have told you my story,—what do you think of it ?"

" Perhaps you would not care to hear, my dear Lady Kynnaston," replied Adelaide.

" Tell me, nevertheless," said her friend, " but I wish you would not call me 'Lady Kynnaston,' Adelaide,—call me Geraldine."

" Well then, Geraldine, why did you not listen to Mr. Latimer ?"

" *Then* I could ,not,—I only thought of Maximilian."

" But now, *now* when you have, as you say that you have, acknowledged to yourself, how right was all he said to you, is there nothing to be done?—Ought not Sir Thomas——,"

" Do not speak of it, Adelaide!" interrupted Lady Kynnaston, vehemently.—" I must entreat his forgiveness,—confess myself in the wrong,—I cannot do it.—Besides, he might not wish it himself, he said, ' upon his *own* account he wished us to separate."

" Oh, Lady Kynnaston!"

" I tell you, Adelaide, I cannot!—It is too late now.—Things must take their course, and the blame must rest with those whose falsehood have occasioned the misery! —Say no more.—Though I asked for your opinion, I do not want your advice.—Will you have the goodness to ring the bell; the fire is going out."

Adelaide rose to obey her with a feeling of despair. What hope could there be of bending such pride as this? Sickness seemed to have had but a transient effect upon Lady Kynnaston's mind; and her temper to recoil and become as stubborn as ever after the momentary relaxation which suffering and reflection had occasioned.

The maid who answered the bell, brought a letter at the same time for her mistress.

" It is from Mr. Latimer !" exclaimed she, when she had opened it ; and after hurriedly glancing through it, told Adelaide that he was coming early next week, to pay her a visit of a few days.—" He desires to be kindly remembered to you," added she.

" I shall be so glad to see him again !" exclaimed Adelaide.

" Will you give the necessary orders, Adelaide dear," said Lady Kynnaston, who appeared to have recovered her composure, " and now pray go out; you have been in this hot room quite too long."

CHAPTER XIII.

AND what had Mr. Latimer been about all this time? After his departure from Bury Hill, he returned, as he had proposed, to College, hoping by means of mental occupation to get the better of his attachment, and recover the cheerful tone of mind habitual to him. But college was empty, for the vacation was not yet over, and there was no absolute and imperative call upon his energy and attention; and while sitting in his solitary study, that attention was perpetually disturbed from the Plato he was annotating, by a bright and youthful countenance which haunted him continually, and which he found it impossible to banish from his memory.

It was of no use. He threw up his books in despair, and determined to make a tour on the Continent, in the hopes that change of scene and the excitement of travel might afford him that distraction which he sought in vain from his library.

Before leaving England he visited Lady Kynnaston to transact some necessary business with her, on the behalf of her husband. It may be imagined why he avoided all mention of Adelaide.

Upon his return to Athens, from an excursion which he had been making in Asia Minor, he found a letter from Mrs. Willoughby, dated some time before, which informed him of what had occurred between Adelaide and Captain Mostyn; of the final separation which had been the consequence, and also of Adelaide's departure, and engagement with Lady Kynnaston.

Joy, at first, overcame every other sensation, at this intelligence,—joy, that Adelaide was still unmarried; that he might yet love her without a crime! and hope, which he had persuaded himself was long since dead, revived with a vigour of which he was hardly conscious. But these feelings

were soon succeeded by the most generous
compassion for the pain which he felt sure
Adelaide must have endured; for he judged
of her affection by his own; and he longed
indignantly for the right to revenge Captain Mostyn's conduct.

The Midsummer vacation was now nearly
over, and Latimer hastened back to England to be in time for Michaelmas term.
He was, therefore, unable to pay Lady
Kynnaston a visit until the beginning of
the third week in December, when he wrote
to give notice of his intended arrival, as
has already been mentioned.

It was with mingled feelings of intense
pleasure and nervous anxiety that he
alighted at Lady Kynnaston's house; and
his heart beat fast as he remained in the

drawing-room, hoping, yet almost dreading, to see Adelaide enter every moment with Lady Kynnaston.

The door opened; Adelaide entered alone; and approaching him with a smile of un-affected pleasure, held out her hand to him with the utmost frankness and cordiality, saying,

"Mr. Latimer! I am so *glad* to see you."

Latimer could only return the pressure of her hand with a few unintelligible mur-murs, whilst his face grew crimson; but Adelaide did not perceive his embarrass-ment, for the evening was rapidly closing in, and its shades stood his friend.

"You must be very cold," said Adelaide, stirring up the fire to a bright blaze. "I wonder you were not frozen to death crossing from Portsmouth such a day as this. Pray sit down in that comfortable armchair; I must play hostess, for Lady Kynnaston is not yet well enough to come down stairs, and she has consigned you to my tender mercies."

"Has Lady Kynnaston been ill?" said Mr. Latimer, almost restored to ease by the playful and almost affectionate cordiality of Adelaide's manner. "I am sorry to hear it. What has been the matter?"

Adelaide gave him an account of her dangerous illness and recovery; of the children's absence; of their discovered relationship; and, in short, of all that it concerned him to know. She then began asking him of his travels and adventures since she had

last seen him ; and they were soon deep in
conversation, which was only interrupted
by the dressing-bell.   Bury Hill was never
once mentioned between them, nor was the
slightest allusion made to any thing which
had occurred during that visit.

Lady Kynnaston, of course, did not come
down to dinner, and Latimer and Adelaide
were again *tête-à-tête.*   How charming he
thought her.   More charming than ever.
Whilst she, in utter unconsciousness of his
feelings towards her, exerted herself to the
best of her ability to make the evening
pass off agreeably.

They took tea in Lady Kynnaston's
dressing-room, who was well enough to sit
up, and receive them there.   Adelaide
thought that her powers of conversation

added still further to the charms of this pleasant evening. Latimer thought he had never been so happy in all his life than when sitting alone with Adelaide, and with no one to speak a word to him but her; and most uncharitably wished that Lady Kynnaston had been a little bit worse, at least for that one evening.

Three or four days passed pleasantly by. Whenever Lady Kynnaston could spare Adelaide from her room Latimer immediately joined her. Lady Kynnaston insisted that Adelaide should walk out, and of course Latimer was her companion. Adelaide was too much of a woman, with all her perfections, not to feel flattered by the pleasure which such a man as Latimer evidently took in her society, and gave

herself up to the pleasure which this friend-
ship occasioned her with the simplest unre-
serve. She had always felt a high esteem
for him since their first acquaintance, and
she now looked upon him almost in the
light of an elder brother. She felt, as it
were, *grown up to him* since their last
meeting, and no longer considered him in
the more awful light of an uncle; while
Latimer himself was too happy in the confiding regard which she made not the
slightest attempt to conceal she felt for
him, to dare to risk forfeiting it for the
chance of substituting a warmer feeling.
He, therefore, studiously avoided any mani-
festation of a tenderness which might have
alarmed her, though often his self-command
was sorely taxed. He would wait, he

thought,—patiently wait,—till he could discover whether her affections were again in her own power to bestow, before he made any demand upon them on his own account.

"When do you think Lady Kynnaston will be well enough, or inclined, to give me an audience upon some business matters?" said Latimer, one afternoon, to his companion, as they were taking their usual walk together.

"Any time, now, I should think," replied she; "and I do wish, Mr. Latimer, you would take the opportunity of speaking to her, to beg her not to have the children home just yet. Scarlet fever is such an insidious malady; and I know that the infection lasts so long. I have said as much myself as I thought advisable, but she told me I knew nothing about it,—that she was the best judge, and that I need not fear but she would take all the necessary precautions; so, what more could I say?"

" I am afraid, when once she has made up her mind, it will be useless attempting to persuade her to alter it. She is, with all her charming qualities, the most inflexible character I have ever met with."

" Do you think," asked Adelaide, presently, " that nothing will ever bring on a reconciliation between her and her husband ?"

" I fear not ; at all events not while her disposition remains as it is at present ; and little short of a miracle can effect an alteration."

" We must make some allowances for her education, and for the bad effect which the faults of others have had upon her disposition; do not you think so?" said Adelaide.

"You know her history, then," said Latimer, in some surprise, "and the unhappy cause of the separation!—Yes, I will make all allowances for the disappointment of her life; but still, be the faults of her parents what they may, that was no excuse for the ungovernable pride which led her, for the sake of revenge, to engage in a marriage in which her heart had no part; and without the least intention of fulfilling any of the solemn promises she made at the altar. Her whole married life has been one long infidelity to her husband."

" Infidelity ! — Oh, Mr. Latimer !" exclaimed Adelaide.

" Yes, Adelaide, infidelity.—Her whole
heart and thoughts were devoted to another,
and I can look upon her conduct in no
other light."

" But you should remember, though I do
not mean to defend her conduct, that her
affections were *first* given to that other.
When she found out the deception that
had been practised upon her, they only *reverted* to that first object, who had never
deserved—as she had been made to believe,
—to lose them."

" I understand what you mean, and can
agree with you so far as this: that her conduct would have been still more reprehensible had she formed the attachment to

Count L—— *after* her marriage instead of *before* it.—What I most condemn is the having entered into that marriage at all; fully aware, as she was, that her affection was not in her own power to bestow with her hand."

" Yes,—but she thought she loved Maximilian no longer; and had he *really* deserted her, most probably she would soon have forgotten her early attachment, and lived very happily with Sir Thomas."

"Possibly; nay, most probably, she might," replied Latimer. "But surely, Miss Lindsay, you cannot palliate that want of candour—I will not call it *dissimulation*—which led her to conceal the whole matter from her husband."

" I think and hope that I should have done otherwise," said Adelaide ; "but no one knows how they may act till they are tried : besides, my disposition is naturally very open ; I do not think I *could* have a concealment from any one with whom I were brought into very intimate relation, if I was to try; but Lady Kynnaston's disposition is reserved, and ———"

"And very proud," added Latimer. "You are an excellent advocate in your cousin's favour ; but if you knew Sir Thomas, as I do, all your sympathies would be enlisted upon his side."

"Indeed, I have the greatest sympathy for him. I feel the pain he has suffered to have been most undeserved, and that he merited a far happier fate ; and I do think my cousin's conduct, not only in this, but in other points, by no means exempt from

blame. But I am so sorry for her!—
She must ave suffered so much!—I can
understand . . . . ."

Adelaide checked herself, and Latimer
made no reply, but amused himself by
striking with his stick at the branches of the
brushwood, which overhung the hollow lane
through which they were walking.

They went on in silence for some little
time, each of them deep in thought; till
Mr. Latimer said suddenly, in an accent
half assertive, half interrogative,

"I suppose there is no such thing as
second love?"

"If that were the case," replied Adelaide,
laughing, "I fancy there would be very few
marriages."

"No,—but I do not mean those fancies,

more or less deep, that people imagine to be
love as long as they last ; I mean, that
when a person has really and truly loved,
it is impossible that. they can form another
such attachment again, should anything interfere with the first.—It is a great pity
people have not two hearts," added he, half
bitterly ; and then, as Adelaide made no
answer, he said, as he switched off the red
berries from a hawthorn branch, that crossed
his path—

"What do *you* think, Adelaide ?"

"About what ?" asked she.

"About what I was saying just now."

"I think," said she, half reluctantly, and
in a voice rather lower than usual, "that
the difficulty would be to distinguish between
the *real* love and the imitation ; and I think

that nothing would prove the *genuine* so much as the inability to form a second attachment, which you mentioned."

Again they walked on in silence, which this time Adelaide was the first to interrupt.

"If you have an opportunity," said she, "pray, Mr. Latimer, say something to my cousin about the imprudence of having the children home again just yet—in spite of all the precautions she has taken, I feel afraid."

"I will, certainly; but I know it will be of no use," replied he.

They now reached the house, and Latimer, requesting Adelaide would ask Lady Kynnaston whether she were inclined to give him an audience, went into the library, while Adelaide ran up stairs to her cousin's dressing-room.

She gave Latimer's message, and was sent down again to beg he would come up whenever it was convenient to him.

He lost no time in availing himself of the permission, and in half an hour joined Adelaide in the drawing-room.

"Well, Mr. Latimer," said she, "what about the children?"

"She has sent for them, and expects them in another hour."

"No!—has she indeed?—I am very sorry!" exclaimed Adelaide.

"We must hope for the best now," said Latimer.

CHAPTER XIV.

THE children arrived; and as soon as they were taken out of the carriage ran into the drawing-room together; Clara, in silent joy; Thekla, in an outburst of riotous delight.

Lady Kynnaston was still up stairs; the weather was so cold that she had not yet ventured to leave her sitting-room. The room in which she had been ill was shut up as a precaution against infection, and she had taken possession of another sleeping apartment. As a still further precaution, she had determined that the children should not approach her for another week : they were only to see each other at a distance.

" Where's mamma ?—where's mamma ?" cried Thekla, extricating herself from Adelaide, who had taken her in her arms to embrace her, while Clara held fast by the skirt of her dress, and gazed in her face with inexpressible affection.

" You shall see her directly, darling," said Adelaide. " You know she has been very ill, and you must be very quiet."

" No, but I want to see her—I will see her !" cried the little rosy cherub ; and I will make a great noise, if she doesn't come directly."

"Oh, Thekla!" said her sister. "You must be good : poor mamma!—May we go to her ?—We will be *so* quiet."

Latimer now came forward, and taking Thekla by the hand, endeavoured to draw her towards him; but the little lady shook him from her, exclaiming,

"I don't want *you*!—I want mamma!"

She did not appear to recollect him ; but Clara, who had fixed her eyes upon him, from the moment he had come forward, now let go her hold of Adelaide's dress, and, running to him, exclaimed eagerly, seizing hold of his hand,

"Where's my papa ?—Have you brought him ?"

"No, dear child," said Latimer, kindly stroking her hair, "he is not here."

"But have you seen him?—Is he coming soon?" cried the little girl, with eagerness still more anxious.

"Not yet, I am afraid, my dear."

The poor child turned away.

"My papa will never, never come," said she; "he told me he would, but he never will." And the tears which gathered in her eyes fell in large crystal drops upon the fur about her throat.

Adelaide and Latimer were both affected at the little girl's distress, and were endeavouring to console her, when the lady's-maid came to summon the children to their mother.

Adelaide led them from the room to the

sitting-room up stairs, which lay at the end of a long passage. The door was wide open, but at its entrance a chair was laid down to prevent the little ones from running in. Within stood Lady Kynnaston, impatiently awaiting their appearance.

When they saw their mother both the sisters released themselves from Adelaide's hold, and rushed forward.

"Stop, children!—children!" cried Adelaide. "You must not get over the chair!—you will frighten mamma!"

Clara obeyed her warning and stopped short at the barrier; but Thekla was over it in a moment, and running to her mother, clasped her little arms around her; at the same time, throwing back her head, her hat fell off, and her flaxen curls streamed back from her ivory forehead, whilst she gazed in her mother's face, her blue eyes dancing with joy. Lady Kynnaston forgot every thing; and seizing her darling in her arms, clasped her to her heart, and covered her with kisses.

All passed in one moment!—and before Adelaide, who witnessed this brief scene in the greatest alarm, could reach the door, Lady Kynnaston had put the child down on the floor again, and, retreating to the further end of the room, commanded her to leave it.

" Come back!—come back, Thekla!" Cried Adelaide, as she ran forwards; but Thekla would not obey either her mother or her governess; and Adelaide, pushing aside the chair, flew into the room, and seizing the child in her arms, in spite of her passionate remonstrances, bore her away.

But it was too late! The infection had been taken! The symptoms of this dread-

ful malady showed themselves unmistak-
ably the very next evening. Clara also
sickened.

Dr. Fenwick was immediately sent for;
but in spite of all his care the children
grew rapidly worse.

Who shall describe the mother's agony as
she hung over her darling's bed, listening to
the ramblings of her infantine and innocent
delirium; the pretty prattling voice, husky
with the painful sore throat; that clear and
brilliant complexion, clouded with the flush-
ings of the fever?

Clara was also very ill; but her mother
paid little attention to her, and consigned
her to the care of Adelaide; she, indeed,
seldom entered the room where her eldest
lay; and if at the little girl's entreaties
Adelaide would go for her, and bring her to
come and see her, she would inquire coldly

how she felt, and hurry back to Thekla
again, leaving her poor little daughter in
tears at her indifference.

The fourth day Dr. Fenwick pronounced
little Thekla's state to be one of great
danger, and told Adelaide that if her father
wished to see her alive he should be immediately sent for.

Adelaide hastened to Mr. Latimer with
this intelligence, and begged him to decide
upon what was to be done.

" The Doctor had better mention it himself to Lady Kynnaston," exclaimed he,
"it will be by far the best plan !"

And he flew to the door to stop him. He
was just in time. Dr. Fenwick re-entered
the house; and the state of the case being
hastily explained to him, he returned to
Thekla's room. " I am come back, for one
moment, my dear lady," said he, in the kind

manner habitual with him, "to urge you to send for Sir Thomas, if within reach ; and that immediately.—He will wish to see his little girls, and I fear," added he, taking her hand, with the kindest sympathy expressed in look and tone, "that you will need a husband's consolation." Lady Kynnaston turned deadly pale, and her fingers grasped the edge of the mantel-piece near which she stood.

"Will you send Adelaide to me, if you please?" said she, making a violent effort to speak.

Dr. Fenwick left the room, and was quickly succeeded by Adelaide. Lady Kynnaston was now seated by the head of the child's bed.

"Adelaide," said she, in a low and husky voice, "Dr. Fenwick has told you—"

"Yes, dearest Geraldine."

"Will you ask Mr. Latimer to be so good as to write to Sir Thomas to tell him?—He is at Southampton, I believe. Send a servant immediately with the letter."

Adelaide hastened to Latimer, and gave him the message. A servant was speedily upon the way to Southampton with a note, conveying the intelligence of his children's danger.

Adelaide was sitting that evening, as usual, in Clara's room. She had hushed the child to sleep; and withdrawing softly from the side of the bed, had just seated herself opposite the fire with a book in her hand, when the door opened, and Lady Kynnaston came in, with such an expression of blank despair upon her countenance that Adelaide started to her feet in alarm.

"Adelaide!—Come!"—gasped she, and hurried away without another word.

Adelaide flew after her, and reached the door of Thekla's room, which stood wide open, immediately after Lady Kynnaston had entered it.

Morland was supporting the little sufferer in her arms, who seemed gasping for breath; her lips, parched and dry, were open, and her brow suffused with crimson, her eyes fast closed. Lady Kynnaston took her child from the nurse's arms, and clasped her own round the tiny form whose head, shorn of its flaxen curls, rested upon her shoulder.

She said not a word, but gazed upon the face of her child in speechless agony. Adelaide and Morland stood round the bed, expecting every moment to hear the last struggling respiration. Tears flowed down the old woman's face, which she kept wiping with the corner of her apron.

"Can nothing be done, Morland?' whispered Adelaide.

."Nothing, my dear young lady! The doctor told me nothing could save her!" and her tears flowed faster than ever; "but we have sent for him."

Five minutes of anxious suspense, which seemed to them an hour, when Thekla opened her eyes; she looked upwards at her mother's face and smiled, and then said, "Mamma!"

"My darling!" exclaimed the mother, "what is it?"

"Love Clara!—Kiss me, mamma."

This was the last word she spoke. Her struggles returned with renewed violence. Doctor Fenwick arrived in another hour, only in time to see her expire.

Hardly had he left the room when Adelaide heard the sound of wheels rapidly approaching the house; there was a loud ringing at the door bell; there was a confused noise of opening doors and hurrying footsteps in the passages. Lady Kynnaston seemed also to hear the sounds, for she started from the bed, where she had thrown herself, though still in silence, upon the body of her child, and stood, with her eyes fixed upon the door.

The door opened, and a gentleman rushed in, his face convulsed with grief, followed by Latimer.

On reaching the bed he flung himself on his knees at its side, and after one glance at the little corpse cried, with a heart-rending expression, while he buried his face in the coverings,

"My little, lovely child!—Oh, I am too late!—too late!"

There was a pause—a silence—only interrupted by the ill suppressed groans of the unhappy father.

At length he rose to his feet. His wife was still standing, pale and speechless, at the head of the bed. Their eyes met—Sir Thomas held out his arms. She made a movement towards him, and was clasped in his embrace; while the tears so long restrained burst their boundary, and sob after sob convulsed her form.

Adelaide and Latimer exchanged glances of heartfelt satisfaction, and instinctively quitted the room together.

She went to Clara's room, Latimer following, and entering it with her. He remained standing at the fire-place, while she stepped softly to the little bed, and gently drew aside the curtains. Clara was in a deep and tranquil slumber.

"How is she?" inquired Latimer, as she returned to the fire-place.

"Thank Heaven! she is going on as well as possible!" and then, referring to the scene they had just witnessed, she said, "Oh, Mr. Latimer! I am so glad!"

He took her hand, and silently pressed it. She did not withdraw it, but continued, as she looked up in his face, with her own artless and confiding expression,

"It seems strange to say so, immediately after the departure of that darling child; but still, I think, one ought not to regret her death, if that alone could purchase the union of her parents—I feel, had she been old enough to understand, she would herself have willingly paid the price;—and then, one is so sure of *her* happiness, little,

innocent angel!—But what will become of
my poor Clara?"   Adelaide's tears now fell
fast, and she withdrew her hand from
Latimer's to raise her handkerchief to her
eyes.

"Consider, dear Adelaide, that this loss
may be the means of the greatest benefit
to her also.   The affection of a mother will
compensate for a sister's love; and I cannot
doubt but that Lady Kynnaston will return
to *all* her duties.—I have the brightest
hopes for the future, and true it is that
there is One who can bring good out of
what we, in our short-sightedness, consider
evil.—I doubt whether any dispensation
less severe than the one which has been
dealt to her, could have crushed that
pride which has been hitherto the bane of
your cousin's life—the source of all her
wretchedness!"

They remained in silence, for Adelaide's heart was so full of conflicting emotions, joy at the reconciliation, grief for its affecting cause, and anxiety as to how poor Clara would bear the intelligence of her sister's death, that she could make no reply.

In a little while the door opened, and Sir Thomas entered the room with Lady Kynnaston upon his arm; her eyes were swollen with weeping, and those of her husband bore also evident tokens of a like emotion.

"She is much better!" said Adelaide, anticipating their inquiry, "and is now fast asleep—I think she had better not be disturbed to-night."

"I will only look at her for one moment," said Sir Thomas.

"Thank Heaven, my Geraldine, we have one still spared to us!" he fervently added, as he softly withdrew the curtain, and looked at the slumbering child.

The poor mother's tears broke forth afresh, and her husband led her from the room.

Latimer exchanged another look of intense gratification with Adelaide.

" My poor friend !" said he, " happiness is still in store for him—and well does he deserve it !"

" And for her also," replied Adelaide.

" And for her also," said Latimer. " She will find that she can love a second time.— But is there nothing but death that is able to destroy a first attachment ?" He stirred the fire gently, as he spoke, and made the remark as if soliloquizing ; but his heart almost ceased beating as he awaited anxiously her reply.

" Yes,"—said she—" Loss of esteem ! —That is more fatal than death !"

He glanced at her quickly, for she spoke almost bitterly, and her face grew crimson; she turned away as if she was looking for something to screen her cheek from the glow of the blaze which Latimer had just made; and then added, as if recovering herself, while she held a newspaper she had taken up from a table beside her, rather shielding her countenance from him than from the fire, "At least I should think so— should not you?"

"It ought," replied he—and he sighed; for though her answer was so inexpressibly agreeable to him, it pained him to think that her feelings were still so sore upon the subject which he felt too surely had dictated her reply. He would have had her indifferent—as long as she was not perfectly indifferent—as long as she had any feelings whatever remaining, connected with her attachment to

Mostyn, who could answer for what the ultimate consequences might be?—And he thought of Lady Kynnaston and Maximilian.

"Tea is ready, if you please, Miss," said the nursery-maid, opening the door.

Births, deaths, and marriages; nothing disturbs the meals of the day. The routine of life rolls round in its daily course, and whether hearts are breaking for grief or dancing for joy, it is supposed their owners must always eat.

"I shall not leave Clara," said Adelaide. "I should be afraid she might awake, and be abruptly told of her father's arrival—but do not you stay, Mr. Latimer."

He would willingly have remained, but could think of no excuse for doing so, and left the room after bidding her good night.

END OF VOL. II.

Lightning Source UK Ltd.
Milton Keynes UK
UKHW041412270119
336297UK00009B/312/P